Meredith Webber lives on the sunny Gold Coast in Queensland, Australia, but takes regular trips west into the Outback, fossicking for gold or opal. These breaks in the beautiful and sometimes cruel red earth country provide her with an escape from the writing desk and a chance for her mind to roam free—not to mention getting some much needed exercise. They also supply the kernels of so many stories that it's hard for her to stop writing!

Also by Meredith Webber

The Sheikh Doctor's Bride
The One Man to Heal Her
The Man She Could Never Forget
A Sheikh to Capture Her Heart

The Halliday Family miniseries

A Forever Family for the Army Doc
Engaged to the Doctor Sheikh
A Miracle for the Baby Doctor
From Bachelor to Daddy

Discover more at millsandboon.co.uk.

FROM BACHELOR TO DADDY

BY

MEREDITH WEBBER

MILLS & BOON

Published in Great Britain 2018
by Mills & Boon, an imprint of HarperCollins*Publishers*
1 London Bridge Street, London, SE1 9GF

ISBN: 978-0-263-93336-9

This book is produced from independently certified FSC™ paper
to ensure responsible forest management.
For more information visit www.harpercollins.co.uk/green.

Printed and bound in Spain
by CPI, Barcelona

For the real Xavier and Hamish,
the two latest wee additions to our family.

CHAPTER ONE

EMMA CRAWFORD LOOKED anxiously out the kitchen window as she added milk to two small bowls of cereal. Above the tree-line she could see smoke growing thicker but the latest news broadcast had assured her that the bushfires raging through the national park on the outskirts of Braxton were still many miles away, and the town itself wasn't in danger.

Bushfires were the last thing she'd considered when she'd agreed with her father that a return to the town where he'd been born and grown up would be a good thing. Being able to bring up the boys in a country town had seemed like a wonderful idea, but it had been the thought of the spacious old home, recently left to her father by an aged aunt, that had held the most appeal.

Well, that and a kernel of an idea that had been germinating deep inside her…

Forget that for the moment! The move had been practical and that was what was most important.

City living was all very well, but the prices in Sydney had meant the four of them—her father, the two boys and herself—had been crammed into an apartment that had shrunk as the babies turned to toddlers—growing every day.

No, Braxton, with its district hospital willing to offer her a job in its emergency department, the surrounding national park, a beautiful beach an hour's drive away, and best of all the rambling old house in its magical, neglected gardens just perfect for two adventurous little boys, had been extremely appealing.

And they had bushfires in Sydney, too, she reminded herself, to shake off the feeling of foreboding the smoke had caused.

She deposited the bowls of cereal on the trays of the highchairs and smiled at the angelic faces of her three-year-old twins, Xavier and Hamish. *She* was off to work and it was her father who'd be cleaning up the mess that two little horrors could achieve with bowls of cereal.

A quick kiss to each of the still clean faces, a reminder to be good for Granddad, a kiss for her father, as ever standing by, and she was gone, her stomach churning slightly at the thought of the day ahead. Although she'd already spent a few days at the hospital, meeting staff and watching how their system operated, this was her first official work day.

'It's called plunging right in,' Sylvie Grant, the triage nurse on duty, told Emma when she arrived. 'The fire turned back out Endicott way and some of the firefighters were caught. It's mostly smoke inhalation—their suits keep them well protected these days. This one's in four.'

Emma took the chart and headed to the fourth curtained cubicle along the far wall, surprised to find the occupant was a woman.

'Your working hours must be worse than mine, especially at this time of the year,' she said, when she'd introduced herself.

The woman smiled then shook her head, pointing to her throat.

'Sore?' Emma asked as she checked the monitor by the side of the bed. Blood pressure and heart rate good, oxygen saturation normal, though the oxygen tubes in the woman's nose would be helping there…

'Let's look at your throat,' she said, using a wooden spatula to hold down the tongue so she could visually check what she could see of the pharynx.

'I can see why it's painful to speak,' she told her patient. 'You've had cold water?'

The patient nodded.

'No difficulty swallowing?'

Another nod.

'Okay, then I'll sort out a drink with a mild topical anaesthetic that should dull the pain, but don't try to talk. The hot air you breathed in obviously reached as far as your larynx so it's likely your vocal cords are swollen.'

She explained what she needed to the nurse, wrote it up on the chart with instructions for it to be given four-hourly and was talking to the patient via questions and nods when Sylvie came in.

And the day became just another day in an emergency department—a child with an ear infection, a woman with chest pains that turned out, after an ECG and blood tests, to be a torn pectoral muscle, a child from the school who'd fallen off a swing and gashed his forehead—stitches and possible concussion so she'd keep him in for observation—an elderly man with angina…

Until, at about two in the afternoon when, as often happened in an emergency department, the place emptied out and one of the nurses suggested they all take a break.

Well, all but Sylvie, and a nurse who'd come on duty for the swing shift.

Emma said goodbye to the firefighter, whose husband had arrived to take her home, and made her way to the small room they all used for breaks, coming in as Joss, one of the nurses she'd met the previous day and also on swing shift, bounced in through another door.

'Hot goss!' Joss announced, grabbing the attention of the three women already in the room, while Emma fixed herself a cup of tea and pulled a packet of sandwiches from the small fridge, pausing to listen to the tale.

'I had dinner last night at the top pub so had a front-row seat to the drama. You know that librarian from the school Marty's been seeing?'

All faces turned expectantly towards her, heads nodding.

'Well, they're sitting at the bar, obviously having words, and then she stood up, slapped his face, and stormed out.'

'Another one bites the dust,' Angie, the department secretary, said. 'Wonder who'll be next.'

They all turned to look at Emma, who had settled into one of the not-very-comfortable chairs and was enjoying her sandwich—especially as she wasn't expected to share it with two small boys.

Joss shook her head.

'No way! You know he stays away from hospital staff, besides which Emma's small and dark, and Marty's preference is for tall blondes.'

'I'm not a tall blonde and I went out with him for a while.' This from a complacently pregnant red-haired woman Emma hadn't seen before.

'That's Helen,' Angie told her. 'She's on the swing shift too, but comes in early to eat our sandwiches because she's always hungry.'

'Not true,' Helen said, although she *was* eating a sandwich. 'It's just that Pete can drop me off so I don't have to drive, and as for Marty, everyone who goes out with him knows the score. He's quite open about not wanting a permanent relationship and if you look around the town most of the women he's been out with are still friends with him. In fact, it was Marty who introduced me to Pete.'

Emma, although curious about this Marty—maybe he

was a GP who did visits at the hospital—turned to Helen, asking when the baby was due.

'Another three months and I'm already so uncomfortable I wonder why I thought it was a good idea.'

She paused, then added, 'You've got twins, is that right?'

'Small town,' Joss explained when Emma looked surprised, but she smiled and agreed she did indeed have twins.

'Three years old, and wild little hooligans already. I'm just lucky I've got my father to help with them.'

'He minds them while you're at work?' Helen sounded slightly incredulous as she asked the question, but Emma just nodded.

'Even does night duty when I'm on night shifts,' she said.

She didn't add that it had been her dad's idea she have the children—well, *a* child it had been at that time, having two had been a surprise.

Dad had taken very early retirement when she'd all but fallen to pieces—well, *had* fallen to pieces—after Simon had died, moving in with her and becoming, once again, a carer to her—a role he'd first taken on when she'd been four and her mother had walked out on the pair of them.

A pang of guilt—one she knew only too well—shafted through her. Dad really should have a life of his own…

Perhaps here…

Soon…

But the conversation was continuing around her and she tuned back into it to find the women discussing unmarried men around town who might suit her.

She shouldn't have been surprised. The remark earlier about her being a possible candidate for the unknown Marty's new woman told her they already knew she was a single mother—single being the operative word.

Small town, indeed.

But before she could protest that she didn't want to go out with anyone, the chat swerved off to the fire. Joss lived out of town on a cattle property and although they were always prepared, she thought this time they'd be safe. She was explaining how they kept the paddocks close to the house free of trees or tall grass when Sylvie came to the door.

'Emma, you're needed on the chopper. It'll put down here to collect you. You have about ten minutes. You know where the landing pad is?'

Emma nodded confidently in answer to Sylvie's question but inside she felt a little nervous. Although, as an emergency department doctor in a small town, she knew she'd be on call for the search and rescue helicopter, and she'd been shown over it by one of the paramedics, she hadn't had much time to take it all in.

By which she really meant she'd refused to think about it. She'd done the training originally to help her overcome her fear of heights, and although she knew most rescue crews got an adrenaline rush at the thought of a mission, her rush was more one of trepidation than anticipation. Yes, she could do her job and do it well, but no amount of training or practice would ever stop the butterflies in her stomach as she waited to hang in mid-air, suspended from a winch.

'—party of older children with special needs from the unit at the high school,' Sylvie was explaining as they left the room together. 'They were walking the coastal path, just this end of it. Apparently, the wind turned suddenly and the fire came towards them, so you can imagine the panic. We know one child with asthma is having breathing difficulties. No idea about the others but they're stuck where they are and will have to be evacuated.'

Beach rescue, no winch!

Her tension eased immediately…

Even inside the hospital Emma could hear the helicopter's approach and hurried to collect the black bag that held all the drugs she could possibly need. But she checked it anyway, relieved to see a spacer for an asthma inhaler, a mask for more efficient delivery of the drug, and hydrocortisone in case the child was badly affected.

Outside, she waited by the building until the bright red and yellow aircraft touched down lightly. Then, ducking her head against the downdraught from the rotors, she ran towards it.

The side door slid open and an unidentifiable male in flight suit and helmet reached out a hand to haul her aboard. She'd barely had time to register a pair of very blue eyes before she was given a not-so-gentle nudge and told to take the seat up front.

She clambered into the seat wondering where the air crew were, but there was no time to ask as the man was already back behind the controls, handing her a helmet with a curt 'Put it on so we can talk', before lifting the aircraft smoothly into the air.

Emma strapped herself in, settled the bag at her feet and pulled on the helmet with its communication device.

'I'm Marty,' her pilot said, reaching out a hand for her to shake. 'And I believe you're Emma. Stephen told me to look out for you.'

'Stephen?' She had turned towards him and shaken his hand—good firm handshake—but wasn't able to take in much of the man called Marty. Unfortunately, checking him out had diverted her from working out who Stephen might be.

'Stephen Ransome—he was up a couple of months ago to introduce the family to Fran. He's my foster brother. You know he got married?'

Steve Ransome was this man's foster brother? Why?

How? Not questions she could ask a stranger so she grasped his last bit of information.

'No, I didn't know, but I'm so pleased. He's a wonderful guy and deserves the best.'

'He is indeed,' Marty agreed, and Emma turned to look at him—or at what she could see of him in his flight suit and helmet.

Tanned skin, blue eyes, straight nose, and lips that seemed to be on the verge of smiling all the time.

So, this was Marty, subject of the hot gossip and, apparently, the local lover-boy!

Foster brother of Steve, who ran an IVF clinic in Sydney and had been her specialist when she'd decided to use Simon's frozen sperm to conceive the boys.

Simon…

Just for an instant she allowed herself to remember, felt the familiar stab of pain, and quickly shut the lid on that precious box of memories.

She was moving on—hadn't that been another reason for the shift to Braxton?

Marty was saying something, pointing out the path of the fire, visible in patches where the smoke had blown away.

She glanced out the window as he manoeuvred the controls to give them both a better view, then straightened up the chopper, intent on reaching their destination.

Marty, the man who didn't do commitment and was open about it…

As she mentally crossed him off her list—not that she had a list as yet—she wondered why he'd be so commitment-shy.

His growing up in a foster family might be a clue.

Had he been born in a disruptive, and possibly abusive, family situation?

That last could make sense…

But he was talking again and she had to concentrate on what he was saying, not on who he was or why he wasn't into commitment, although that last bit of info was absolutely none of her business.

'There's a coastal path that runs for miles along most of the coast in this area, and people can do long walks, camping on the way, or short walks,' he explained. 'The school mini-bus dropped these kids about five miles up the track—there's a picnic area that's accessible by road—and the idea was they'd walk back to Wetherby and be picked up there. It's a yearly tradition at the school, and the kids love it. Unfortunately, the wind spun around from northeast to northwest and the fire jumped the highway and raced through the scrub towards the path.'

'Poor kids, they must have been terrified,' Emma said. 'Do we know how many there are?'

'Two teachers, a teacher's aide, and sixteen children,' Marty said grimly. 'Hence no aircrew. We stripped everything not needed from the chopper because we'll only have two chances to lift them all off the little beach they ran to. Once the tide comes in, that's it, and not knowing the age or size of the kids makes calculations for lift-off weight difficult.'

Emma nodded. She'd learned all about lift-off weight during the training she'd undertaken in Sydney, necessary training as the rescue helicopter at Braxton relied on emergency department doctors on flights when one might be needed.

They were over the fire by now, seeing the red line of flame still advancing inexorably towards the ocean, while behind it lay the black, smouldering bushland.

Two rocky headlands parted to give a glimpse of a small beach and as they dropped lower she saw the group, huddled among the rocks on the southern end, their hands held protectively over their bent heads as the down-thrust from the rotors whipped up the sand.

'Good kids, did what they were told,' Marty muttered, more to himself than to Emma.

They touched down, the engine noise ceased, and before she could unstrap herself, Marty was already over the back, opening the doors and leaping down onto the sand.

He turned to grab Emma's bag then held up a hand to help her down. An impersonal hand, professional, so why didn't she take it? Jumping lightly to the sand as if she hadn't noticed it…

'I'm a trained paramedic so if you need me just yell,' he was saying as she landed beside him. 'I'm going to juggle weights in the hope we can get everyone off in two lifts.'

He paused and looked her up and down.

'You'd be, what—sixty kilos?'

'Thereabouts,' she told him over her shoulder, hurrying towards the approaching children. One of the adults—probably a teacher—was helping a young, and very pale, girl across the beach.

'Let's sit you down and make you comfortable,' Emma said to the child, noting at the same time a slight cyanosis of the lips and the movement of the girl's stomach as she used those muscles to drag air into her congested lungs.

'I'm Emma, and you're…?'

'Gracie,' the girl managed.

'She's had asthma since she was small but this is the first time we've seen her like this,' the woman Emma had taken for a teacher put in.

'Do you have your puffer with you?' Emma asked, and was pleased when Gracie produced a puffer from a pocket of her skirt.

'Good girl. You've had some?'

Gracie nodded, while the teacher expanded on the nod.

'She's had several puffs but they don't seem to be helping.'

'That's okay,' Emma said calmly to Gracie. 'I've brought a spacer with me, and you'll get more of the medicine inside you with the spacer. Have you used one before?'

Another nod as Emma fitted the puffer to the spacer and inserted a dose, then found a mask she could attach to the spacer so the girl could breathe more easily.

'Just slow down, take a deep breath and hold it, then we'll do a few more.' Probably best not to mention twelve at this stage. 'See how you go.'

The girl obeyed but while it was obvious that the attack had lessened in severity, she was still distressed.

Marty had appeared with the oxygen cylinder and a clip and tiny monitor that would show the oxygen saturation in the blood. He joked as he clipped it on the girl's finger, and nodded to Emma when the reading was an acceptable ninety-four percent.

The oxygen cylinder wouldn't be needed yet.

Emma drew the teacher aside and explained what had to be done to fill the spacer and deliver the drug.

'Are you happy to do that on the way to the hospital?' she asked, and the teacher nodded.

'I do it all the time,' she said. 'My second youngest is asthmatic. We just didn't think to carry a spacer with us.'

Which left Emma to fill in the chart with what she'd done, dosage given, and the time. The flight from the hospital had only taken fifteen minutes so the child would be back in the emergency department before there was any need to consider further treatment, and she knew from her briefing that another doctor would have been called in to cover for her.

Marty had done a rough estimate of the weight of his

possible passengers and had begun loading them into the helicopter. To the west the smoke grew thicker and the fire burning on the headland to the south told them they were completely cut off.

He looked at the tide, encroaching on the dry sand where he'd landed. He had to move now if he wanted to get back here before the tide was too high.

'I'm taking the sick child and the teacher with her,' he said to the new doctor, wondering how she'd cope being left on the beach surrounded by fire on her first day at work.

'And the teacher's aide who's upset,' he added, concentrating on the job at hand. 'She's not likely to be of any use to you, plus another six children. Will you be all right here until I get back? You have a phone? We're quite close to Wetherby so there's good coverage.'

'I have a phone, we'll be fine, you get going,' she said, waving him away, and as he left he glanced back, seeing her hustling the children towards the sheltering rocks to avoid the sand spray at take-off.

Sensible woman, he decided. No fuss, no drama, she'll be good to work with.

He settled the asthmatic girl in the front seat and strapped in those he could, letting the rest sit cross-legged on the floor.

He ran his eyes over them, again mentally tallying their combined weight, adding it to the aircraft weight so he was sure it was below take-off weight. The next trip would be tighter.

They were off, the children sitting as still as they'd been told to, although the urge to get up and run around looking out of windows must have been strong. The teacher he'd brought along would have sorted out those who were strapped in seats, he realised when the excited cries of one child suggested he had at least one hyperactive passenger.

'Can you manage?' he asked the teacher, who was in the paramedic's seat behind the little girl, and had put another dose of salbutamol into the spacer and passed it to his front seat passenger.

'Just fine,' the sensible woman assured him. 'You fly the thing and I'll look after Gracie. Deep breath now, pet, and try to hold it.'

The school mini-bus was waiting behind the hospital as he landed, and the aide helped the children into it while the teacher took Gracie into Emergency.

'Most of the parents are at the school,' the bus driver told him. 'I'll take this lot there, then come back.'

Marty nodded, hoping he hadn't misjudged the tide and that he would be bringing back the other children, the teacher and the unknown Emma Crawford.

As *yet* unknown? he wondered, then shook his head. Hospital staff were off limits as far as he was concerned.

Besides which, she was short and dark-haired, not tall and blonde like most of his women.

Most of his women! That sounded—what? Izzy would say conceited—as if he thought himself a great Lothario who could have whatever woman he liked, but it really wasn't like that. He just enjoyed the company of women, enjoyed how they thought, and, to be honest, how they felt in his arms, although many of his relationships had never developed to sexual intimacy.

What colour were her eyes?

Not Izzy's eyes, obviously, but the short, dark-haired woman's eyes—the short, dark-haired woman who wasn't at all his type.

The switch in his thoughts from sexual intimacy to the colour of Emma Crawford's eyes startled him as he flew back towards the beach.

Meanwhile, the woman who wasn't at all his type was attempting to calm the children left on the beach. Three were in tears, one was refusing to go in the helicopter, and the others were upset about not being in the first lift. The teacher was doing her best, but they were upsetting each other, vying to see who could be the most hysterical.

'Come on,' Emma said, gathering one of the most distressed, a large boy with Down's syndrome, by the hand, 'let's go and jump the little waves as they come up the beach.'

Without waiting for a response, she steered the still-sobbing child towards the water's edge, and began to jump the waves herself. A few others followed and once they were jumping, the one who still clung to Emma's hand joined in, eventually freeing her hand and going further into the water to jump bigger waves.

'Now they'll probably all compete to go the deepest and we'll be saving them from drowning,' Emma said wryly to the teacher, who had joined her at the edge of the water.

'At least they've stopped the hysteria nonsense,' the teacher said. 'They work each other up and really…' She hesitated before admitting, 'I was shaken by it all myself, so couldn't calm them down all that well.'

'No worries,' Emma told her. 'They're all happy now.'

Which was precisely when one of them started to scream and soon the whole lot were screaming.

And pointing.

Emma turned to see a man race down the beach and dive into the water, her fleeting impression one of blackness.

'He was on fire,' one of the children said, as they left the water and clustered around their teacher, too diverted by the man to be bothered with screams any more.

Emma waded in to where the man was squatting in the water, letting waves wash over his head, her head buzzing with questions. How cold was the water? How severe his burns? Think shock, she told herself. And covering them…

'Can you talk to me?' she asked, and he looked blankly at her.

Shock already?

'I'm a doctor, I'd like to look at your burns. I've got pain relief in my bag on the beach.'

She touched his arm and beckoned towards the beach but he shook his head and ducked under the water again.

Time to take stock.

He was young, possibly in his twenties, and very fair. His hair was cut short, singed on one side and blackened on the other. The skin on his face on the singed side was also reddened, but not worse, Emma decided, than a bad sunburn.

If the rest of his body was only lightly burned then maybe waiting in the water for the helicopter was the best thing for him. She tried to see what she could of his clothes—now mostly burnt tatters of cloth. At least in the water they'd have lost any heat they'd held and not be worsening his injuries.

But shock remained an issue…

'Can I do anything?' the teacher called from the beach.

'If you've got towels you could spread a couple on the beach—just shake any sand off them first.'

Not that shaking would remove all the sand, but if she could get him out, lay him down and cover him loosely with more towels, she could take a better look at him and position him to help with possible shock.

The low rumble of the helicopter returning made them all look upward, and Emma was pleased to see the children running back to the rocks.

Pleased to think she could avoid the difficulty of examining him here on the beach, she was also relieved to have help getting the man out of the water.

'Rescue helicopter,' she told him, hoping the words might mean something. 'It will fly you to hospital.'

This time she got a nod, but as she reached out to take his arm and help him to stand upright, he pulled back again.

She didn't argue—he was probably better staying where he was rather than risk getting sand on his burnt skin.

Marty saw the two heads bobbing in the water below him and wondered what was happening. At least the kids were all over in the rocks.

He hovered for a minute before touching down, checking the seemingly minute area of sand that was still above the incoming tide. It would have to be a really quick in and out.

As soon as he jumped down, the children hurtled towards him, all talking at once. Jumping waves, man on fire, doctor might drown…

He thought the last unlikely but had pieced together the information by the time the teacher arrived to explain.

'He won't come out,' the teacher told him. 'And every time Emma tries to take his arm, he dives away from her. He might be a foreign backpacker and not understand she's trying to help him.'

Marty nodded.

Most of the backpackers roaming Australia had some knowledge of English, but the shock of being caught in the fire could have been enough for this poor bloke to lose it. He pulled a couple of space blankets out of the helicopter and gave them to the teacher to hold.

He turned to the kids.

'Now, all of you sit down on the sand, and the one sitting the stillest gets to fly up front with me, okay?'

The children dropped as if they'd been shot and although Marty doubted they'd stay still long, it should be long enough to get Emma and the man out of the water.

And work out what he was going to do next.

Maybe the man was very small…

Emma had apparently finally persuaded her patient to move towards the shore so Marty had only to go into knee-deep water to reach the six-foot-plus young man.

'I haven't been able to get a good look at his burns but I'd say some of them are serious,' Emma told him, her face pale with worry about this new patient.

She took one of the space blankets from the teacher, who had unfolded the silver material, and wrapped it around the man's shoulders, looking across him so Marty saw the worry in her serious grey eyes.

Grey, huh?

'I'll give him some morphine for the pain, and start a drip.' She turned to the teacher. 'Could you manage the fluid bag on the trip back to the hospital? It's just a matter of holding it above his body and making sure the tube doesn't kink.'

'And just why are you asking that?' Marty demanded as they both helped the man into the chopper and settled him on the stretcher.

She turned and touched his arm, just above the wrist—a simple touch—getting his attention before saying very quietly, 'Because there's no way you can take him *and* me, given how tight your take-off load was already. I'll just wait until the tide goes down and someone can come for me. I'll be all right, although you'll have to phone my dad and let him know what's happening.'

Marty stared at the small hand, still resting on his arm, then studied the face of this woman whose touch had startled him. She met his gaze unflinchingly.

'Well?' she said, removing her hand and concentrating again on their patient.

He shook his head, unable to believe that she'd figured all this out and delivered it to him as naturally as she might tell someone she was ducking out to the shops.

'That's right, isn't it?' she continued, as she calmly inserted a cannula into the man's undamaged hand and attached a line for the fluid. 'The children are upset already, so the teacher has to go back with them. I'm the obvious choice to give up a place.'

'And you're happy to stay alone on the beach?'

Grey eyes could flash fire, he discovered.

'I didn't say I was happy about it, but as I can't fly the helicopter I can't see any other solution. You'll have some chocolate bars in the helicopter—I've never been on one that didn't—so you can leave me a couple, and some water. I'll be fine as long as you phone my dad.'

Much as he wanted to argue, there was little point. He couldn't take off with both of them on board—not safely…

He went with practical.

'There's a cellphone signal here, you can phone your father yourself.'

It seemed a heartless thing to say to a small woman he was about to leave on a deserted beach with bushfires raging all around her, but his mind wasn't working too well.

Something to do with grey eyes flashing fire?

Impossible…

She half smiled as she drew up a calibrated dose of morphine and added it to the drip.

'I could if my phone hadn't been in my pocket when I went into the water.'

'Well, of all the—'

He stopped. Of course, she wouldn't have considered her phone when there was a man in the water who needed her help.

Realising she was so far ahead of him he should stop talking and just do something, he wetted some cloth with sterile water and laid it over the man's legs where the stretcher straps would go, so the burns wouldn't be aggravated.

Or too aggravated.

He tilted the stretcher to raise the patient's legs, then checked on the children—all of whom were still sitting remarkably motionless on the sand near the door.

'Okay, you stay,' he said to Emma, 'but I'll be back for you just as soon as I can. Are you winch trained?'

'I am, but I don't think that'll be possible tonight. Even if you're still on duty, the chopper will be needed to get the young man to a burns unit,' she told him. 'I'll be fine. It's warm and there's enough soft sand on the top of the dune that will stay dry so I can sleep on that until someone can get back here. Or if the fire dies down, I can walk out.'

Could he read the nonchalant lie on her face? Emma wondered as she satisfied herself that their patient would make it safely to Braxton Hospital, where he'd be stabilised enough for a flight to the nearest burns unit.

But it wasn't really a lie. The twins would be fine with her father, they were used to her coming and going, but—

Damn her phone!

Damn not thinking of it!

'Here's a spare phone and an emergency kit. Chocolate bars and even more substantial stuff, water, space blanket, torch.'

She spun towards Marty and read the worry in his face as he handed her the phone and backpack. He was hating doing this, leaving her on her own on the beach, but he was a professional and knew it was the only answer.

'I'll be back for you,' he said, touching her lightly on the shoulder, and this time she didn't argue, backing away towards the rocks to avoid the rotor-generated sandstorm.

CHAPTER TWO

AS THE LITTLE aircraft lifted into the air, she watched it until the noise abated, aware all the time of the part of her body his hand had touched.

It had to be caused by comfort for some kind of atavistic fear, she decided. A reaction to being left so completely alone in a place she didn't know at all.

Ring Dad.

Speaking to her father calmed her down. As ever he was his wonderful, patient self, assuring her the boys were already eating their dinner, having had a busy day helping him in the garden.

Emma laughed.

'I can just imagine their idea of helping!'

'No,' her father said, quite seriously. 'Once I'd explained which were weeds to be pulled out and which were plants to be left behind, they only removed about half a dozen chrysanthemums that needed thinning anyway, and one rather tatty-looking rosemary that looked as if it was happy to give up the struggle to live.'

There was a pause before her father added, 'But more importantly, what about you? You're out near the coast path? I saw on TV that the fire had swung that way.'

'I'm on a beach, and quite safe. I've even had a swim.'

She told him about the man in the water and made light

of being left behind, doing her best to give the impression she wasn't alone.

'I'm just not sure what time the chopper will be able to get back,' she told him, 'so I may not be home before morning.'

For all Marty's 'I'll be back' she just couldn't see it happening. The dune at the top of the beach might still be dry, but it would be impossible to land anything bigger than a drone on it.

She spoke to both the boys, who were full of their gardening exploits, then said goodbye.

An emergency telephone would be kept fully charged, but it was not for idle chatter. Who knew when she might need it again?

Marty delivered his passengers to the hospital, following the stretcher with the burns victim into Emergency. He'd radioed ahead to make sure there was a senior doctor on duty, and was relieved to see Matt, another of the chopper pilots also there on standby.

'I'll do the major hospital run,' he told Marty. 'You've had enough fun for one day.'

As he'd spent hours this morning helping out with water bombing the fire, Marty knew his official flying hours were just about up. But his day was far from finished. He left the hospital, getting a cab back to the rescue service base where his pride and joy was kept—his own, smaller, private helicopter.

A quick but thorough check and he was in the air again, this time heading for the seaside town of Wetherby. The man he and all his foster siblings called Pop had levelled a safe landing area for him behind the old nunnery that had housed his foster family, and within ten minutes he was home.

Home. Funny word, that—four small letters but, oh, the massive meaning of it, the security it held, the memories…

Hallie was first out through the back garden to meet him, Pop emerging more slowly from his big shed. Both of them were older now, well into their seventies, but still fit and healthy, always ready with help or advice, or even just a cup of tea. They had been the first people in the world to offer him love—unconditional and all-encompassing love—and were still the most important people in his life.

He lifted Hallie in the air and swung her around, explaining as he swung that he couldn't stay. He'd left a woman on Izzy's porpoise beach and had to get her off while the tide was still high enough to take the jet ski in.

'What jet ski?' Hallie demanded. 'You boys took all your fast, noisy toys when you left here.'

He grinned at her.

'The jet skis at the surf club are bigger, stronger, and faster than any we ever had, poor orphans that we were!' he said, unable to resist teasing her. 'I've phoned a mate to have one fuelled up for me.'

'You're going around there on a jet ski in the middle of the night.'

He had to laugh.

'Hallie, it's barely seven o'clock. We'll be back before you know it. I'll take her straight to Izzy and Mac's as she'll need a shower and some dry clothes. Something of Nikki's will probably fit her. There's not much of her.'

'Then bring her here for dinner when she's dry,' Hallie insisted, but he shook his head.

'She has her own family to get back to,' he said, 'but we have to come back here to get the chopper so I'll introduce you then.'

He turned to Pop.

'Okay if I take your ute down to the club?'

'Just don't run into anything,' Pop growled, and they

all laughed as the ute was ancient and, having survived numerous teenagers learning to drive in it, was a mass of dents and scratches.

Down at the club, while his mate checked the fuel on the jet-ski, he called the emergency phone, and knew from Emma's voice when she answered that he'd startled her.

'It's okay, it's only me, Marty. I'm coming to get you and want you to stand in the middle of the beach and point the torch that's in the emergency kit straight out to sea so I don't run aground on the rocks.'

Silence on the other end told him she didn't know what to make of these instructions, but the jet ski motor was on and he had to get going, this time while the tide was high, not low.

'See you soon, don't forget the light,' he said, and disconnected.

Fortunately, the sea was calm, as it often was when a westerly had been blowing across the land. But his heart raced as he thought of the woman he'd left on the beach—standing there in the darkness, the world behind her ringed with fire. Surely she'd be...

Frightened?

The thought made him smile. He might not know Emma Crawford very well—not at all, in fact—but he doubted fear would be upmost in her mind.

Apprehension, yes, but fear?

He revved the engine, anxious to get to her—frightened or not, it must be an unnerving experience for her, especially on her first day at work!

Emma stared at the phone in her hand.

Had it really rung?

Was Marty serious about coming in by water to get her off the beach—what little of it was left?

Presumably...

She lifted the emergency backpack he'd left with her, took out the torch, and slipped the pack onto her shoulders. She then paced the beach and decided where the centre of it was, waded in knee deep then turned on the torch as instructed, pointing its beam out to sea.

She was just beginning to feel a little foolish when she heard the loud roar of an engine, definitely somewhere in the darkness of the ocean, then light appeared, at first shining across the width of the bay, the motor throttling back but still very loud in the otherwise silent night.

Now the light turned towards her and, as if drawn along the path of torchlight, a large jet ski rumbled her way, the noise cutting as it approached so it drifted right up to where she stood.

Marty was off in an instant.

'On you hop,' he said cheerfully, while she was still considering what seemed like a miracle night rescue.

'Quickly—we need the tide high now,' he added, holding the craft steady in the small waves while she clambered on board.

'Now shove back to make room for me, then hang on tight,' he said, and before she could say thank you, or marvel at the fact that he *had* come for her, he had the craft moving again and they were off, the roaring motor preventing even the most basic of conversations.

But she did hang on tight, very tightly indeed, for they were travelling at what seemed a ridiculous pace, bouncing over waves as they sped back to wherever he'd come from.

Wetherby?

The beach town she and the twins had visited last week?

Was that the closest place?

And was she thinking these thoughts to keep from considering the strange reaction she was experiencing with her arms around a man's body, her breasts pressed against his back—the solidity of it, the different feel…

The maleness…

Not that she'd been clasping a woman's back recently, but there was something decidedly odd going on within her body.

Decidedly odd and totally unnecessary, but just as she considered not holding on quite as tightly, they leapt another wave and her arms tightened around him even more.

Maybe as well as needing a father for the boys, *she* needed a man.

Although friends and relations had been suggesting such a thing for some years now, she'd never given it a thought, probably because she'd never experienced a physical…

What?

She didn't want to call it need, but it was certainly a male-female kind of thing she was feeling right now.

Though this particular man—a commitment-shy lover boy—was definitely not for her.

There was no way she could tarnish the memory of the intense and beautiful love she and Simon had shared with a quick affair to satisfy a…

'Need' did seem to be the word…

Consumed by her thoughts, she was unaware of the silence that had fallen, but the jolt as the jet ski glided up a ramp onto the deck outside the surf lifesaving clubhouse told her the journey was over.

She let go of the body that had started such bizarre thoughts in her head, and dismounted as quickly as she could, although the wet clothes she was wearing made that difficult, sticking to the plastic seat and tangling around her legs.

'Thank you,' she said, as Marty put out his hand to

steady her. 'And for rescuing me as well. I'd have been okay staying there till morning, but Dad would have worried.'

'Only Dad?' Marty queried, and it must have been the tiredness that was creeping over her that stopped her thinking the question at all odd.

'Well, the boys as well, but they've grown up with my erratic hours of work, and my coming and going, and they don't seem to mind. Dad's been there for them far more than I have.'

She'd smiled at him as she'd explained, this small, wet, matter-of-fact woman, and Marty didn't know if it had been the smile or the love she somehow invested in the word 'Dad' that caused an uneasy lurch in his usually reliable stomach.

'This way,' he said, and although he would normally have slung an arm around a woman's shoulders to lead her to the car, tonight he couldn't do it, so he stomped ahead, slightly perturbed, although he didn't do perturbed any more than he did stomach lurches. For most of his life he'd kept his demons at bay by being the joker, the light-hearted mate, just a 'good bloke' in the Australian vernacular…

He grabbed a couple of towels Hallie had thrown into the ute, and handed one to Emma, using the other to dab himself dry before tying it around his waist. Woman-like, she wound hers around above her breasts, though not before he'd noticed the way her wet clothing clung to a very curvy figure.

You like tall, slim, blonde women, don't date hospital staff, and don't do commitment, he reminded himself. And a woman with 'boys' would be looking for commitment. Would need commitment…

'We're both wet through and will be chilled to the bone by the time we get home so I'm taking you to Izzy and Mac's,' he told his passenger. 'Izzy's one of my foster sisters, and Mac, her husband, is the local doctor here in

Wetherby. They actually met at the little cove where we rescued the kids, only they were rescuing a porpoise. Their daughter Nikki is about your size, and should be able to provide some dry clothes.'

Sensible talk—that was the way to handle the strangeness he was experiencing, which, as he now considered it, was probably caused by his having to leave her alone on the beach in the first place. It had brought out all his protective instincts, nothing more…

Izzy, obviously primed by Hallie, had Emma through the door and into the bathroom while he was barely out of the ute.

Mac met him on the wide veranda of the centuries-old doctor's house.

'You can use the back bathroom, I've put some dry duds in there,' he said, waving Marty along the veranda, following to ask about the rescues, about the injuries to the burns victim, the hospital network having already filled Mac in on what had transpired during the afternoon.

'At least the temperature and the wind have dropped,' he said, 'and the forecast for tomorrow is rain, so it should dampen what's left of the fires on the coastal fringe, although those in the national park will be harder to stop.'

'Great news,' Marty replied, pleased to have talk of bushfires diverting his brain from its seeming obsession with Emma. He could do bushfire talk! 'The firefighters will get a break, and with decent rain these might be the last of the fires for the season.'

'Let's hope so,' Mac said. 'I'll leave you to have a shower, then Izzy's made some sandwiches. If you want to get straight back to Braxton you can eat them on the way.'

Marty turned in the doorway of the bathroom that had been tacked onto the veranda at the back of the house.

'Thanks, Mac, I appreciate it.'

Mac smiled at him.

'That's what family's for,' Mac reminded him.

Marty took the words into the shower with him and as the water splashed down over his body he thought of the main one—family. How lucky had he been to have landed with foster parents whose determination had been not merely to provide a home for abandoned or damaged children but to provide them with a family—to meld them into a family in the truest sense of the word—a group where they belonged?

But as he dressed in dry, borrowed clothes, his mind returned to Emma and *her* family—boys, Dad, her—but no wedding ring and no mention of a husband.

Not that it was any of his business, and neither was he interested in finding out more. He tried not to think about the fact that, given the gossip mill that was the hospital, he'd soon know everything there was to know about Emma Crawford, and probably far more than she wanted people to know.

He was smiling to himself as he pushed open the door into the kitchen and greeted Izzy with a kiss.

'No Nikki?' he asked, looking around the room, taking in Emma's appearance in long shorts and a slightly too tight T-shirt, damp dark hair framing her face like a pixie's in a story book.

'Studying with her friend,' Izzy explained. 'Now, Emma's having a cup of tea. Do you want one or do you need to get back to Braxton? I've made sandwiches to go if you can't stay.'

'We'll go but take the sandwiches, not that I expect we'll be able to eat them all because you know Hallie, she'll have a basket of goodies already packed into the helicopter. But thanks.'

He dropped another kiss on her cheek, then bent and kissed her baby bump.

'That's from your Uncle Marty, Bump. I hope you're behaving yourself in there.'

Mac and Izzy laughed, but although Emma smiled, he sensed a sadness in her.

Or maybe it was just plain exhaustion. For a first day at work, it had been a beauty!

'Come on,' he said to her. 'Let's get you home.'

Had he spoken too abruptly—too roughly—that she looked startled and stumbled slightly as she stood up, and her hand shook as she put her cup on the table?

'Are you okay?' he asked, when they'd said their good-byes and were back in the ute.

'Fine,' she said quietly, 'though I'll be happy to get home. It's been a long first day.'

But was she entirely happy to be going home?

Of course she was.

Then why the little niggle somewhere deep inside her that suggested she'd have liked to stay a little longer with Marty's family, sitting in the kitchen, talking about nothing in particular?

She thrust the thought away, aware that it was something to do with being in a new town, and not having had time to make friends, her life revolving around the boys and now work.

'Tired?' Marty asked as they pulled up in the shed behind a huge old building.

'I think I must be,' Emma replied, deciding that would explain all the strange things going on in her head.

'Well, I'll have you home in no time,' he told her as he led the way to where two elderly people waited by a little helicopter. 'Do you have a car at the hospital?'

His hand was behind her back, guiding her through the dark yard, barely touching her, yet the—probably imagined—warmth from his hand was as distracting as the niggle had been earlier.

'Car? Hospital?' he asked again as she didn't reply.

She shook her head, hoping to clear it.

'No, I walk to work.'

'Then I can run you home. The good thing about Braxton is that nowhere's far from anywhere else.'

The small helicopter looked like a toy after the rescue aircraft.

'This is yours?' she asked, glad of distraction.

'My pride and joy,' he told her, 'and the two people standing beside it are my—well, mother and father, Hallie and Pop.'

He introduced Emma, explaining she was new to Braxton.

'I've put a bit of food in a basket behind the seats,' Hallie told them.

'And Izzy packed us sandwiches,' Marty said. 'We might have to stop on the way home for a picnic.'

Everyone laughed, but the picnic idea had taken hold in Emma's head. It was such a short flight back to Braxton, and eating on the way would be awkward.

'If you're driving me home and not in a hurry to get back to your place, we could picnic on my veranda,' she found herself saying as they flew over the mountain range between the two towns. 'The boys will be in bed, and Dad will happily join you for a beer if you fancy one, or a glass of wine if you'd prefer. I think after the day I've had I'll be having one.'

The words rattled out of her mouth, and the pleasure she felt when he agreed was all to do with making friends—well, *a* friend.

And having worked with him and seen him with his family, she knew he'd be a good friend to have.

Or so she told herself.

But he *would* be a good friend to have, an inner voice insisted. Hadn't he introduced one of the nurses to her husband?

Surely she wasn't thinking he might do the same for her? This from the more sensible of her inner voices…

And she didn't really want a *husband*, did she?

The thought reminded her once more of loss and pain—first her mother, then Simon. No, she couldn't go through that again, the pain of loss was just too much to bear. But it *would* be nice to have a father for the boys.

The voices stopped arguing as the helicopter touched down back in Braxton, and Marty transferred wet clothes and the picnic goodies to his four-wheel drive.

Although now a slight uneasiness had crept into Emma's head to replace the argument.

Oh, for heaven's sake! Sensible inner voice to the rescue. You're only going to share a meal with a colleague, what the hell is wrong with that?

'Wow, you live in this place?' Marty said as they drove up the street towards the big house. 'I've often wondered about it because for years it seemed abandoned, then suddenly it came to life again.'

They pulled up outside the old federation house, with its fresh white paint, wide verandas and dark green roof, and Emma saw it through Marty's eyes—the front steps climbing up to the veranda, the wide hall with its gleaming polished floorboards leading off it, living and dining rooms off to one side, bedrooms and bathrooms off the other. And at the end of it the kitchen, already the heart of the home.

'It was Dad's aunt's place and she was ill for a long time before she died. Dad grew up in Braxton—a little further up the hill. The four of us, me, Dad and the boys, had been crammed into a tiny flat in Sydney so when this became available we couldn't move fast enough. I think we'd have come even if I hadn't been able to get the job. Moved here, and just believed something would eventually come up.'

'I doubt any country hospital would turn away a doctor—particularly an ED specialist.'

Having heard them arrive, her father had turned on the light over the front steps and was waiting at the top of them.

'Dad, this is Marty...' Emma stopped and turned to her companion. 'Do you know, I've no idea of your second name. But my father's name is Ned, Ned Hamilton.'

Somehow they sorted out the confusion, Marty supplying an unexceptional surname of Graham, and explaining about the food.

After which, as always seemed to happen these days, Dad took charge, bringing out plates, and napkins, cold beer and a bottle of chilled white wine, a couple of wine glasses dangling precariously between the fingers of one hand.

Emma took her wet clothes through to the laundry and glanced in at the sleeping boys before joining the party. Her father was telling Marty that he was kept fairly busy by the boys during the day but was slowly reconnecting with old school friends.

'The boys will be in kindergarten from the beginning of next term so he'll get more free time,' Emma put in, but her father and Marty had discovered an acquaintance in common. One of Marty's older foster sisters—one of the first children fostered by Hallie and Pop just over forty years ago—had been at school with Ned.

'Carrie has twins too,' Marty said to Ned—and just when had he found out her boys were twins? She tried very hard not to refer to them as 'the twins' as though they were one entity.

She tuned back into the conversation and found that this

unknown woman's twin daughters were in their final year at high school and very experienced babysitters.

'In fact,' Marty said, as Emma poured herself a glass of wine and selected a sandwich, 'I could check whether they're already booked for Saturday week. It's the annual barn dance for the animal shelter just outside town. A barn dance is a bit old hat for teenagers these days so they won't be going to it, but for you, Ned, it would be a chance to catch up with other old school friends, and I'm sure you'd enjoy it, too, Emma. I'd be happy to take you both. I always go.'

Which certainly wasn't a date, Emma realised, while her father was agreeing enthusiastically to this plan, and reminiscing about the good times he'd had at the annual event.

'It's been going that long?' Emma asked, and Marty laughed.

'Your father's not exactly ancient,' he reminded her. He glanced at Ned. 'You'd be, what, mid-fifties?'

'Spot on,' her father replied. 'I took early—well, very early—retirement when Emma needed a bit of help, though for a few years I did a lot of supply teaching, filling in for absent teachers.'

Marty was delving into Hallie's basket as her father explained, and now produced a paper plate piled with homemade biscuits and another with slices of chocolate cake.

'Heavens!' Emma said. 'There's enough food here to feed an army.'

'Or two always hungry little boys who'll love these leftovers.' Her father smiled as he spoke.

'Though, really, Marty should take it,' Emma suggested.

'And deny the boys Hallie's chocolate cake? I think not!'

Laughing blue eyes met hers across the table and for

a moment the air caught in her throat, just stuck there, as if she'd forgotten how to breathe.

Of course she could breathe!

In, out, in, out—simple as that.

But it seemed to take forever to get it sorted…

Not that her absence from the conversation was noticed as her father was now exclaiming about Hallie and Pop still being in Wetherby.

'I met them, you know, quite a few times when I was a member of the surf club, and seeing a bit of Carrie.'

'Small towns,' Marty said, smiling again, but this time, thank goodness, at her father. 'Carrie was one of the first children they took in, she was about twelve at the time so she was their first teenager. My lot—me, Izzy and Stephen, both of whom Emma's met—and a couple of others were the last. I think all of us being teenagers together finally convinced them they'd done enough.'

'What didn't kill them made them stronger,' her father remarked with a smile.

'Dad was a high-school teacher so he knows all about teenagers,' Emma explained, mostly to prove to herself she could speak as well as breathe…

The evening ended with complicated arrangements being made for her father and the boys to meet up with Carrie and her twins, the potential babysitters, and her father walked out to the car with Marty while Emma cleared the table and put everything away.

'Well, that was fun,' her father said, wandering back into the kitchen a little later.

The words sent a sharp pang of guilt spearing through Emma.

'I'm sorry, Dad, I've been so selfish, letting you give up your life to help me out, first when Simon died and I lost the baby, and then with the boys. I hadn't realised quite *how* selfish I've been until tonight.'

Her father put his arms around her.

'You needed me back then, so where else would I have been? And wasn't it me who talked you into having the boys, and didn't I promise to look after them for you?'

He kissed her on the top of her head, adding, 'And I've enjoyed every minute of it, but tonight, meeting Marty, and sitting out there just talking about nothing in particular, has shown me how restricted our lives have become. That was natural when the boys were small and very demanding, and the flat was really no place to be entertaining, but we both need to get out a bit more now, and the barn dance is a splendid idea.'

He was voicing the feeling she'd had back at Izzy and Mac's place—voicing the fact that their lives had become too constrained, too centred around work and childcare.

She moved a little away from him and kissed his cheek.

'You're right,' she agreed. 'It's time for both of us to get out and about. Who knows what's waiting for us out there in the wild country town of Braxton?'

Her father chuckled and they parted for the night, Emma going quietly into the boys' room and watching her sons sleep for a few minutes before dropping a kiss on each of their heads and taking herself off to bed.

Where, exhausted as she was, sleep was a long time coming.

Mainly because every time she closed her eyes she saw an image of a pair of laughing blue eyes.

She'd no sooner banished this image—with difficulty—when the barn dance hove into her mind. Though with Dad going too, the gossip mill could hardly slot her into the ranks of one of 'Marty's women'.

Could it?

CHAPTER THREE

IT WAS SOMEWHERE during this mental argument that she fell asleep, to be woken by two very excited boys telling her God had brought them a puppy.

'We've been praying and praying,' Xavier was saying, while Hamish, usually the leader, echoed the words.

'Praying and praying?' Emma muttered weakly, then remembered the playgroup her father and the boys had attended at a local church in Sydney.

But praying for a puppy?

It was the first she'd heard of it!

The boys were now bouncing on her bed so any thought of going back to sleep was forgotten, while their combined pleas to come and see it dragged her reluctantly out of bed.

The 'puppy', sitting quietly in the kitchen listening to a lecture from her father on a dog's place being in the yard, was the size of a small pony. It leapt up in delight when it saw the boys and lolloped towards them.

And her, where it slobbered enthusiastically all over her pyjamas.

However, that gave her more time to check it out. For all it had, at some time, been well cared for, it was painfully thin and none too clean.

'Sit,' she said, and was surprised when he obeyed immediately. He'd definitely been cared for by someone who'd taken the time to train him.

But a dog?

A strange dog?

'I think we should leave him outside until he's had a bath,' she said, which brought wails from both boys.

'Well, go and play with him on the veranda,' she compromised, following them as far as the door so she could keep an eye on all three of them, mainly the dog.

'We can't keep him,' she said to her father over her shoulder. 'He'll just be something else for you to look after. Besides, he's sure to belong to someone. We can take a photo, put up posters, maybe ring the local radio.'

Her father nodded.

'I'll do all that, and I'll take him to the vet, get him checked out. He might be micro-chipped. But if no one claims him, well, the boys do love him already and he'd be great for them. I've been watching him closely and he's certainly not dangerous. The yard's all fenced and he's big enough to handle two rough little boys.'

Emma shook her head, then realised the dog had taken up far too much time already and if she didn't hurry she'd be late for work.

But a dog?

Were they settling in to country life so quickly?

The ED was quiet when she arrived, not quite late but close, and the chat about the triage desk was of the forthcoming barn dance—apparently one of the big events in the Braxton social calendar.

Maybe the animal shelter would take the dog.

She was about to ask when the radio came on—an ambulance ten minutes out. Sylvie lifted the receiver to her ear so the whole room didn't have to hear, relaying information to Emma as it came through.

'Atrial fibrillation, blood pressure not too bad but pulse of one hundred and forty.'

Emma's mind clicked into gear. Amiodarone drip. The

cardiologist she'd always worked with recommended an initial IV treatment of one hundred and fifty mg over ten minutes, followed by sixty mg an hour over six hours and thirty mg an hour over eighteen hours.

But…

'Is there a local cardiologist?' she asked Sylvie, although she was reasonably sure the town would be too small to support one.

'No, but we have a fly-in-fly-out cardio man. He does two days a week in his office in Retford, then flies around about six country towns each fortnight. We usually phone him with any problems, and, without checking to be sure, I think he's due here tomorrow.'

Emma nodded. Presumably she could phone him, as she'd have done in the city, although down there the specialist she'd phoned had usually been in the same hospital or in rooms close by. It was strange the shift from a huge city hospital to a small country one, but the work remained the same.

'Could you get him on the phone for me?' she asked Sylvie as she walked away to meet the ambulance and its passenger.

'It happens every so often,' the patient told her cheerfully, obviously unfazed by the sudden onset of fibrillation. He was a man in his late thirties or early forties, she guessed, and sensible enough to know when he needed medical help.

She walked with the trolley into a cubicle and asked Joss to help their new patient into a gown then get an ECG started, a blood sat clip on one finger and a cannula in his arm.

'Do you see the visiting cardiologist?' she asked her patient, now introduced as Rob Armstrong, who nodded, while Joss bustled about, sticking pads for the electrodes on the man's body.

Sylvie walked in with a phone in her hand, and Emma moved outside the cubicle to take the call.

After introducing herself, she told him about the patient, whom he apparently knew quite well.

'And what would you do?' he asked, and she felt a rush of pleasure. Many specialists would simply dictate their preference.

She told him what she'd do, and was even more delighted when he said, 'Well done, you! I love knowing efficient ED doctors. It makes for a far better outcome for the patient. Go ahead exactly as you thought, and I'll be there tomorrow. Unfortunately, he's got one of those stubborn hearts that will probably need cardioversion to shock it back into normal rhythm but we always try the drugs first. It's up to you, and available bed space, but I can do the cardioversion in the ED if you decide to keep him there.'

A few pleasantries, a promise from him to phone later for a report, and he was gone. A nice man, Emma decided. She'd look forward to meeting him.

In the meantime, she had a patient to see to. Joss had already taken a list of the medications he was on, and Emma was pleased to see blood thinners on the list.

'We need to take some blood for testing before we attach the drip, and a chest X-ray—'

Damn, she hadn't asked the specialist if he wanted an echocardiogram as well.

Decided to leave it. She'd ask him when he phoned and could do it then if he wanted one.

She wrote up the details of the drug delivery, and, as a radiographer came in with the portable machine, she explained it to Joss.

'No worries,' Joss assured her. 'I've been here long enough to have seen Mr Armstrong a few times now. He's lucky the cardiologist is coming tomorrow. When he can't have the cardioversion within forty-eight hours, he has to go on drugs to keep him as stable as possible for about a month, not that he complains.'

She hesitated and Emma had a feeling she was being assessed.

'Actually, he's a great guy, Rob Armstrong—that's our patient—he's an engineer with the local council. Single too.'

Emma frowned at the nurse.

'And I might be interested in that information, why?'

Joss wasn't the least abashed by Emma's cool demand.

'Oh, just that you're single, and those boys of yours—well, I think boys probably need a father, you know, to kick a football around with and stuff—so I was just saying...'

'Take blood for testing then start the drip,' Emma told her, but Joss's smirk suggested she hadn't spoken nearly sternly enough.

Because that little seed of an idea that the boys might need a father had been slowly spreading its roots in her mind?

Because she'd found meeting men in the city fraught with danger and doing just that had been one of the reasons she'd been happy to move to Braxton?

So what if it had been? She was fairly certain it wasn't written across her forehead.

And she certainly wouldn't be eyeing up patients as prospective husbands—very unethical—although in a small town most of the men she was likely to meet would be prospective patients!

Yet here she was, on only her second day at work, with someone doing a bit of very unsubtle match-making.

And adding to her confusion over what exactly she did want in the future...

Seeking distraction, she phoned Retford Hospital to enquire about the man with the burns.

He was doing well, she was told, mostly second-degree burns, and he'd now been identified and a friend tracked down. He was, as she'd suspected, a backpacker, walking the track on his own after his friend had picked up casual work at the last village they'd visited.

The person on the other end of the phone already knew who she was—did small town gossip travel from town to town so quickly?—and enquired how she was enjoying Braxton, laughing when Emma explained it was only her second day.

But the conversation made her feel…as if she belonged? As if she'd somehow come home?

Weird!

Not that she had time to consider the strange feeling of belonging, for the day got busier, with a farmer coming in with the skin on his left hand lacerated from being caught in a baling machine he was fixing.

'Not an everyday thing in a city hospital, I bet?' he said to her as she cleaned the wound and stitched the tattered skin back together.

'No, it's not,' she agreed, but it wasn't only the type of accident that was different. The man's cheerful good humour was like the friendly phone call she'd had earlier. Somehow people seemed to have more time to chat, or perhaps felt freer to talk than they did in the city.

From time to time she checked on Mr Armstrong, but she had no time to think about the man as anything other than a patient.

Although he *did* have an engaging grin, and the kind of rugby-player build that made her think he probably *could* kick a ball.

Not that ball-kicking ability would have been top of her list of desirable qualities in a father for the boys—

Not that she had a list.

But as she walked home later that day, she was slightly startled to find herself thinking about a list. Well, not actually a list but what she *might* want to consider necessary attributes in a father for her boys.

Was she being silly, thinking this way?

Had growing up without a mother—wonderful though Dad had been—sown the seed about wanting a father for the boys?

But a father for the boys would also be her husband.

Was she ready for that?

For love?

Because, in all fairness, that's what it would need to be…

She shrugged off the thought and had got to the gate before she'd reached any conclusion in the matter.

And now the 'puppy' was stopping her, standing behind the gate so she had to shove hard to open it, reminding it that this was her home not his.

'You're just passing through,' she told him firmly, as he showed apparent delight at her return by standing on his hind legs to lick her cheek.

'Here, boy!'

The male voice that wasn't her father's startled her, but the dog must have heard authority in it for he immediately stepped back from her before gambolling away towards the house.

Emma was moving in that direction herself when clear shouts of 'Mum, look at us,' had her turning towards the big mango trees that lined one side fence.

When she'd left for work the previous day, her father had been in the process of assembling a double swing set. She'd arrived home in the dark last night but now she could see what the excitement was about.

'It's like seeing double,' she said as she walked towards

the trees where two identical teenage girls were pushing two small, identical boys.

'These are our friends,' Xavier told her.

'They're called Milly and Molly,' Hamish added.

The two girls laughed.

'Mandy and Molly,' one of them explained. 'I'm Mandy.'

'And I'm Molly.'

They'd stopped pushing the swings and moved towards Emma, holding out their hands as they introduced themselves.

'Marty thought you might be looking for babysitters—well, *a* babysitter but we come as a pair, although we don't charge double.'

Molly—or it might have been Mandy—was explaining this but Emma's brain was still getting over a jolt of recognition. It had been Marty's voice that had called 'Here, boy'—Marty Graham, who didn't do commitment so certainly wouldn't make even a secondary list for a possible father for her boys!

But if his voice was here, so must he be.

The girls were pushing the swings again, so there wasn't anything to keep Emma under the mango trees.

Nothing at all—

'Emma, I've made a fresh pot of tea.'

Her father's voice this time.

She had to go and join him and…

Well, whoever was with him.

Yet try as she might, she couldn't figure out the reluctance that weighed her down as she made her way towards the house.

Marty stood as she approached the table.

'Have you had a busy day?' he asked, and she heard sincerity in his voice. But it wasn't the tone of voice or even the words that held her in limbo on her approach to the table.

Something else—something she didn't understand—had stopped the world for a moment. She could see the low table set with tea things and leftovers from Hallie's basket, with another chocolate cake added to the feast. And there was a woman, sitting smiling at her, speaking words Emma couldn't hear.

Because of Marty?

Couldn't be!

He took her elbow, leading her forward, introducing her to his sister Carrie, mother of the babysitting twins, and probably maker of the new chocolate cake.

Marty dropped his hand, and the world righted itself again, so she was able to smile at Carrie and tell her how happy the boys seemed to be with her girls.

'But it's a bit of a shock,' Marty said, his blue eyes smiling at her in a quite unnecessary way, 'seeing the four of them together. I thought I was seeing double—which I suppose I was—but it was weird.'

'Exactly my reaction,' she told him, but switched her attention to Carrie as she spoke so she didn't have to dwell on the blue eyes.

Dwelling on blue eyes was a definite danger—she knew that as certainly as she knew her own name, even if she had no explanation for the knowledge.

'Tea?'

Her father held up the fresh pot and Emma nodded, taking the chair Marty had pulled closer to the table while she was battling to stay focussed. Carrie was telling her how amazing it had been to meet up with Ned again and, glancing at her father, Emma rather thought he considered it special as well, for he was smiling at the attractive, dark-haired woman as she spoke.

Emma settled back in the comfortable cane chair her father had inherited with the house, and sipped her tea. It was a pleasant, unexpected distraction after a busy day, but seeing her father chatting away to their visitors, she felt again the stab of guilt that the demands of the boys had kept him from the normal social interaction a retired man might expect.

Especially a younger retired man…

Not but what bringing her up had probably stopped any normal social interaction long before she'd had the twins…

She finished her tea and stood up, intending to take her cup to the kitchen, explaining she'd better start on the vegetables for the boys' tea.

'Sit down,' her father said—not quite an order but close. 'And leave the cup, we can sort it later. I've already asked Carrie and Marty to stay for dinner—we'll have a barbecue. I bought lamb chops and sausages today and you can throw a salad together while I cook.'

'I'll give you a hand, Ned. I love a barby,' Marty said, and as he pushed back his chair and moved away from the table, Emma dared a sneak look at him.

It wasn't that he was drop-dead handsome or even, to her way of thinking, all that sexy, but something about the man drew her to him.

The lure of the unattainable?

Was it easier to moon over someone totally unsuitable than to go through the 'getting to know you' procedure with another man? Was that what was causing her uneasiness over Marty?

Uneasiness?

Yes, uneasiness! She was damned if she was going to call it attraction.

'Don't you agree?'

She came out of the fuzz in her head and was wondering just what Carrie had been saying to her when her phone buzzed.

'Sorry,' she said to Carrie. One glance told her it was the hospital, and as she stood up and moved a little apart to take the call, she saw Marty walking back around the veranda.

'Duty calls,' he said, waving his phone at her.

'I'm wanted too,' Emma told him, before heading for the kitchen to tell her father.

Marty watched her slip away before hurrying down the front steps and out to his car.

Should he wait for her?

Offer to drive her?

It would be no trouble to drop her back later…

He heard her voice and saw her out in the yard now, saying goodbye to the two little boys, thanking Carrie's girls for playing with them.

'Are you on duty for the chopper?' he asked as she came towards him.

'Seems so,' she said. 'Traffic accident on some road I've never heard of so I'm glad you're the pilot, not me.'

She smiled at him and he knew the blip in his heartbeat was something he had to ignore. For all he'd been startled by his reactions to Emma, she wasn't for him. A woman with children needed commitment…

'I'll give you a lift to Base,' he said, mainly to show the blip and his other reactions they didn't matter and that he could be in her company without ever thinking of her in a non-platonic way.

Perhaps.

'The hospital will have sent whatever supplies you'll need straight to the chopper,' he added persuasively, although he knew he should be organising things so he saw less of her, not more.

She studied him for a moment—a fleeting moment—then shook her head.

'I'll need my car to get home,' she told him in a voice that suggested it was the end of the conversation.

'I'll drive you home, it's no bother. If we're in the same car we can pool whatever we've been told about this accident and maybe work out how we're going to tackle it.'

He wasn't really holding his breath, but when she nodded her agreement, the relief that swept through him suggested he might have been.

'I was told it was a traffic accident,' she said, as they pulled away from the house. 'The driver's badly injured and is still being cut out of the car.'

She paused, then asked, 'Wouldn't an ambulance have been just as quick?'

He glanced towards her, glad she was already mentally attuned to the situation, as he should have been. But, no, he was taking the opportunity to study her.

Just briefly!

Study her and wonder just why she affected him the way she did—this small, quiet woman.

Looking at her didn't help, so he turned his thoughts firmly to what lay ahead.

'With badly injured patients, we often just grab and go. Stabilise them as much as possible but get them into the air and en route to a major hospital as quickly as we can. That's why we take a doctor, so you can work on the patient while we're in the air. Statistically, it's better for the patient.'

'I hadn't thought of that. In the city, the nearest hospital is usually a major one so it's not an issue. What's the nearest one to the crash site?'

'Retford, a thirty-five-minute flight each way.'

'And if the patient needs better stabilisation than we can do on the ground?'

She was good, this woman, thinking her way through all the possibilities.

'Then it becomes a very long night. We bring him—

or her—but we'll stick to him, to Braxton, stabilise him, *then* take him to Retford.'

They'd reached the base and he was pleased to see Emma out of the car as soon as he pulled up, already hurrying towards the open side door of the chopper. He caught up with her and they jogged over together, Mark, his paramedic air crewman putting out his hand to help Emma up.

'And up front is Dave,' he told Emma. 'These are the best two crewmen in the skies. Mark'll give you a helmet so you can listen to the chat.'

He slid into his seat, his mind now firmly focussed on what lay ahead, Dave giving him the latest information from the crash site, and the co-ordinates he needed.

The big chopper lifted into the air, and the sense that this was where he belonged swept over him. It was here, in the air, that he really lived, the muddy waters of his early years receding like the tide so he was whole again.

He thought of his foster sister, Liane, wondering if she'd had some place she could go where all the past was forgotten. Perhaps if she had, she might have lived.

Dave's quiet voice brought him out of the useless speculation, and now he could see the bright arc lights of the emergency services teams revealing a macabre scene of twisted metal wrapped around a substantial tree.

He put the chopper down as close to the scene as he possibly could. Word had come through that the two passengers in the car had been taken to Braxton by ambulance, both suffering from minor injuries.

But whoever was still trapped inside—well, he didn't want to think about it, because the front of the vehicle had concertinaed and pushed the engine back onto the driver.

A fire officer was using the huge cutters to free the man—his gender confirmed on arrival at the scene. Emma was squatting close by the vehicle, checking what the ambos had already done to help the victim—checking the victim himself as best she could, given that a low, heavy branch of the tree prevented her from getting right up to him.

'We need to hook the rear of the vehicle up to the fire truck and see if we can haul it off the tree,' the fire officer told them. 'Problem is we don't know if it will make things better or worse for him.'

'The way the dashboard has come back on him, there could be injury to the femoral artery on both legs,' Emma pointed out, 'so we've got to be ready for massive blood loss.'

She was speaking to Mark, who nodded his understanding, hauling pads and bandages out of one of the flight bags.

'And hypovolemic shock?' Marty muttered, thinking through what lay ahead, the paramedic he'd once been never far away at the scene of any accident.

'Definitely. But we deal with the normal things, check his airway, immobilise him on the stretcher…' she turned around and nodded when she saw that Dave had the stretcher ready behind her '…put pressure on any wounds to slow the bleeding. I'll start IVs in the air and check him over properly, but getting him to hospital as quickly as we can will be the best thing we can do for him.'

The deep growl of the fire engine made them both step back, and slowly—protesting noisily—the vehicle was dragged away from the tree. Marty moved in to help the fire officers who were still working on freeing the patient, helping them fit a block and tackle to the front of the vehicle, already cut free, so they could lift it off the injured driver.

And Emma was proved correct. As the pressure lifted, blood spurted from the man's thighs. Being closest, Marty clamped his hands against the wounds and held tight until Mark and Emma came with dressings.

'Bind it tightly,' Emma said to Mark, then she half smiled. 'Sorry, telling you something you already knew, wasn't I?'

And while Emma bound the man's other leg, Marty fastened a collar around the man's neck while Dave slid a spine board down behind him. Once strapped to that, Emma was happy for them to lift him onto the stretcher.

'Let's get him airborne,' Marty said, hurrying to the chopper, Mark and Dave following him with the stretcher, while Emma jogged alongside, adjusting the oxygen mask the ambos had fitted.

He had the aircraft ready for lift-off by the time Mark confirmed the patient was secure, and as they rose into the air, he glanced into the rear-view mirror in front of him and saw Emma kneeling by the patient, fitting a cannula into the patient's hand, ready for fluid resuscitation.

All in all, it had been a good grab and go—slightly delayed by the problem of extricating the man but they'd still make it to hospital not far outside what the emergency staff considered the first golden hour.

He felt a sense of satisfaction, although another glance in the mirror—another glance at Emma attending to their patient—reminded him the job wasn't finished.

Not yet.

The flight home from Retford to Braxton was uneventful, and beyond Marty congratulating them all on a job well done, there wasn't much chat.

No doubt, Emma thought, because none of them felt confident about their patient's future. His injuries had been horrific, not only the damage to both legs but internal injuries caused by the steering wheel being driven back into his body.

'I'm glad I'm not in Retford Emergency tonight,' she

said quietly, and while Mark and Dave murmured their agreement, Marty was far more positive.

'At least there they had a full team of trauma specialists standing by and he'll be whisked into Theatre probably before we get home.'

'Is he always this positive?' Emma asked, and Mark and Dave laughed.

'He's the world's greatest optimist,' Mark told her.

'Yep,' Dave added, 'his glass isn't just half-full, it's practically brimming over.'

Why? Emma wanted to ask, but the two crewmen were indulging in a 'remember the time' conversation and she tuned out to think about her own positivity, which she believed was fairly strong.

Except when she was tired, or the boys were playing up, or—

No, she told herself firmly, she was a very positive person.

But driving home with Marty, in the close confines of a vehicle, with whatever it was going on inside her body whenever he was near, she was positively confused.

How ridiculous!

She was tired, probably exhausted, that's all it was.

'You tired?' he said, picking up her thought.

'Not really,' she said, though why she denied it she had no idea.

'Liar,' he said softly. 'I can see your head nodding. You're nearly asleep.'

And whatever restraint she'd been managing to hold onto snapped.

'Okay, I'm tired, exhausted, in fact. There, are you satisfied now?'

'Hey,' he said softly, reaching out to touch her arm. 'I didn't mean to upset you. I was just teasing.'

'Then don't,' Emma retorted, although she rather thought she meant *Don't touch me* rather than *Don't tease.*

'I won't again, I promise,' he said, but as she turned towards him she saw a smile hovering about his lips and knew his eyes would be smiling as well.

What was it with this man, that stirred her up so much?

He pulled up outside her house and she hesitated before opening the door, wanting to make amends for her earlier tetchiness.

'I'm having a cup of tea before I go to bed. I find it relaxes me. Do you want something?'

Idiot!

Fool!

Imbecile!

The words raged through her head, but it was as if this man had mesmerised her in some way.

'I won't, thank you,' he said, and an unlikely feeling of disappointment descended like a cloud.

He was turned towards her as he spoke and she turned her head away, hoping her feelings weren't obvious.

Apparently not because now he was getting out of the car and walking around to open her door. Well, hold the door because she'd managed to open it as soon as she'd realised what he was doing.

She slipped out past him, far too close, said thank you and good night and hurried towards the front steps.

He was waiting by the car, a tingling sensation up and down her spine telling her he was watching her go. Sheer politeness to see she got safely inside, she knew that, but…

She turned at the top of the steps and waved, absent-mindedly patting the dog who'd heard her arrival and come to stand beside her.

Marty waved back and drove off, while she stayed where she was and watched until the two red tail-lights disappeared from view—

To be replaced within seconds by the glare of headlights, and what was unmistakeably Marty's vehicle pulled up in front of her gate once more.

The light was on above the door so she couldn't pretend she hadn't seen him, but as he got out of his car and came purposefully towards her, she felt her heartbeat accelerating as a kind of panic filled her body.

'Something you forgot?' she asked, doing her best to sound at ease.

'Just thought I'd have that cuppa after all. I know we're both tired but we don't have to be up for an early shift, so we might as well relax together.'

The last two words sent shivers through Emma's body, although she knew perfectly well what he meant.

Idiot!

Fool!

Imbecile!

The words ran through Marty's head as he watched Emma bustling about in the big, country kitchen, taking what seemed like forever to make a pot of tea.

Why on earth had he come back?

What had drawn him?

He had nothing to offer this woman, so surely the less he saw of her the better?

Yet the car had barely reached the end of her street before he'd turned back, the fleeting expression of disappointment he'd caught on her face vivid in his mind.

Now he was sitting at the kitchen table while she pushed a cup and saucer, the teapot, milk and sugar, and the remnants of the chocolate cake towards him.

'I'd have thought if your boys didn't finish it off, Molly and Mandy would have,' he said, pouring his tea but waving away the cake. 'Or this "puppy" of yours.'

'Dad's pretty strict about how much sweet things the

boys eat,' his hostess replied politely. 'Especially close to bedtime. And I'm still not sure about the puppy being ours.'

She didn't look at him as she spoke, too busy pouring herself a cup of tea, although how much concentration did that really take?

'He's good with the boys? Your father?'

'The best,' she said, with not a hint of hesitation, but it was there again, a shadow in her eyes, nothing more.

He closed his eyes briefly. Had he turned his car around—come back—for this? An inane conversation with a woman he barely knew?

Not that she was keeping up her end—inane or not. His polite question had been answered—briefly—but she hadn't picked up the conversational ball and lobbed it back to him.

And now, when he looked across at her, she was frowning at him while the dog, sitting like a sentry beside her, studied him closely.

'Why did you come back?' she asked.

He stared at her, willing words to come. Words usually came easily to him, and as for a simple chat over a cup of tea? Well, he considered himself something of an expert!

But how could he tell her he'd seen something in her face, so fleeting he couldn't even be sure it had been disappointment?

Tell her whatever it was had touched him in some way?

'For a cuppa?' he suggested, and tried a smile, but knew it was a feeble effort.

'And?' she persisted.

'I really don't know,' he said, resorting to honesty. 'I just felt we'd parted wrongly, somehow. Felt that I should have had a cuppa with you. I suppose…you're new in town, might need a friend, and I *mean* a friend, nothing more. You've probably heard the gossip—Marty doesn't do commitment…'

Aware he was burbling on, tripping over his words and actually saying nothing intelligent, he stopped.

Emma studied him for a moment, then shook her head, and he read her tiredness in the gesture.

'I'm sorry, you're exhausted. You've had a tough introduction to Braxton. I'll get going—leave you in peace.'

He stood up, drained his cup and set it back down in its saucer.

'But if ever there's anything you need—anything I can do for you—just let me know.'

She half smiled.

'Because Stephen told you to look out for me?'

Relief flooded through him—it was the perfect excuse. Far better than saying, *You looked disappointed that I didn't stay...*

'Of course,' he said. 'But because we're colleagues as well. Up at the hospital, we all look out for each other.'

He could tell by the look on her face that she didn't believe him—well, not entirely—but how else could he explain the uncontrollable urge that had had him turning his vehicle and heading back to her house?

'As I said, if there's ever anything I can do, you only have to ask,' he said, aware that his voice sounded rough.

There was something about this woman…

'Thank you,' she said, oh, so polite, although the words seem to hold—what? Longing?

Definitely something, but what he couldn't define.

He walked down the front steps, feeling all kinds of a fool—coming back the way he had, confused, and slightly unhappy…

'Bye.'

He was at the bottom of the steps now and turned at the word, looking back up at the woman who'd spoken—

at the dog by her side. She raised her hand and wiggled her fingers, and a tension he'd never felt before—or not within recent memory—filled his body.

He was tired, that's all it was.

Yesterday had been a big day, today even longer…

Maybe he was sickening for something.

But as he got into his car and drove away, he knew it was none of these things.

Any more than it was to do with whatever she wanted—or didn't want—to talk about.

This was different, internal somehow.

Emotional?

He was pretty sure it wasn't love, because love didn't—couldn't, surely—happen like that, like a thunderbolt from the blue—but whatever he was feeling was something he'd never felt before.

He loved Hallie and Pop and his foster siblings, but that was different. It had grown almost organically as he'd grown within the family.

Which only went to prove love wasn't thunderbolt stuff.

But whatever it was he *was* feeling, he didn't want to feel now…

Definitely didn't want to feel now!

Of all the women in the entire world he should *not* be getting involved with, Emma was at the top of the list.

Emma had children, and children meant commitment.

And he didn't do commitment—at least in his ramblings he'd managed to tell her that much.

He just couldn't *trust* himself to do commitment.

An image he'd thought he'd banished forever flashed clearly through his mind—not the blow itself, or the blood that had flowed after it, but his father's arm rising, slowly, menacing, then deliberately striking downwards.

His own arm, many years later, rising the same way,

hitting out at the man—barely a man—who'd stolen his girlfriend…

It wasn't the sins of the father handed down, but the genes…

CHAPTER FOUR

THE FOLLOWING DAYS were busy for Emma, but totally Marty-free. Not that she wanted to see the man who was causing so much confusion in her mind and body, but he'd been such a presence in her first few days at work, she couldn't help but be aware of his absence.

Molly and Mandy had called in after school one afternoon to play with the boys, and Emma had to wonder if it had been prearranged when Carrie came to collect them and joined her father for a beer on the veranda before taking them home.

She couldn't feel anything but pleased that her father had found an old friend, and if she wondered, as she lay in bed at night, just how friendly they might have been in the past, she dismissed the thought as none of her business. At least her father was happy…

And her own social life was improving—slightly. She'd had a drink after work on Friday afternoon with Joss and a couple of other staff, Joss suggesting that she bring the boys out to her farm over the weekend.

'We've a couple of orphan lambs and a poddy calf the boys might like to play with,' she'd said. 'Come tomorrow and stay to lunch.'

Knowing the boys would be delighted with the farm animals, she'd agreed immediately, resolutely ignoring an inner whisper that she'd miss Marty if he happened to pop in.

Something he hadn't done for a couple of days, she had to admit.

And why should he?

He'd produced babysitters for her, found a friend for her father to help him settle back into town, and offered her friendship too—what more could she expect?

Nothing.

Why should she?

Especially when he'd made it very plain that friendship was all he would offer.

But when she arrived back from Joss's place, two exhausted boys sleeping in the back of her car, and saw the familiar four-wheel drive parked outside the gate, why did her heart rate rise, while her mind wondered just how much of the farm mud that had liberally covered the boys had ended up on her nose or cheeks?

'Good morning?' he asked, coming down the front steps and offering to carry one of the boys inside for her.

'Great morning, and I can manage,' she said automatically, *and* stupidly as she couldn't manage—not both boys at once—not now they were getting bigger.

As he'd already unhooked Xavier from his car seat and was lifting him out, she hoped her words might have gone unnoticed, although the eyebrow he cocked at her as she leant in to free Hamish told her otherwise.

'Kids look so innocent when they're asleep,' he said quietly as they stood and watched the boys settle into their cots.

'Only if you don't know what devils they can be when they're awake,' Emma told him, although seeing her children sleep always tugged at her heart.

'I suppose,' he murmured.

The whispered words seemed to linger in the air, although they had been spoken as Marty left the room. His tone had been tinged with something she couldn't identify—sadness?

Regret?

She knew from his footsteps he'd walked out onto the veranda and much as she'd have loved to have a shower—or at least check for mud—before she faced him, she knew she had to follow.

Had he a reason for being here?

Was it to do with her?

'You look as if you had a good time,' her father said, running his eyes over her farm-stained clothes.

'The boys just loved it.'

She looked from her father to Marty, who, she rather thought, was also taking in her appearance.

'Did you want to see me?'

Silly question—what if he said, no, he'd just called in to see her dad.

Although her father had already drifted off, no doubt back to the garden that was becoming a passion with him.

'I did,' Marty said, and, no, her heart *didn't* skip a beat! 'I know it's a bit short notice, but the Mid-Coast chopper has offered to cover our area tomorrow and I'd like to do a winch refresher session. I know you're up to date with your winch protocols but our aircraft is new to you and it's possibly a different winch to one you've used before. We'll all be involved and if we can get through it in the one day—maybe even the morning—we're right for six months.'

He paused, as if waiting for some response, but Emma was too busy hiding the dread she always felt about winch work to answer him. Why it still happened when she was extremely proficient at it she had no idea.

'All the crew do six-monthly refresher training,' Marty

continued, 'but we've got out of sync, so if we can all do it together, it'll save having special days for one or two crew members.'

He obviously needed an answer, so Emma managed a nod, then, realising that might be a little wishy washy, went for a word.

'Super!' she said, though it was far from how she felt and was not a word she could recall using before that moment. 'What time and where?'

'Seven, at the base. Best to get started before the wind gets up. We'll just do a lift and lower for each of us and if we've time a quick carry, just clip on and lift then down and unclip.'

He grinned and added, 'Pilots included.'

As if that made it better! Those men threw themselves around in the sky as if it was their playground. Dangling on a rope—well, a wire—thirty, forty, fifty feet above the earth wouldn't bother them at all.

'I'll be there,' she said, then thought of something.

'Can I go first?'

She didn't add, because it would be stillest, instead using the boys as an excuse.

'That way I can get back and spend most of the day with the boys.'

'You could bring them,' the ever-helpful Marty said. 'They might like a flight.'

'No way!' Emma told him, aware of the blood draining from her face at the thought of the boys in a helicopter. Helicopters crashed…

With a promise he'd see her at seven, Marty departed, but not before wondering just how nervous Emma was about her children.

She'd certainly seemed shocked at the thought of him

taking them for a ride, though he knew small boys usually loved being airborne.

Did she worry herself when she flew?

Dislike flying?

If so she'd hidden it remarkably well on the trips they'd already taken together.

Although winch training was always a test of a person's mettle. For someone who didn't like heights or flying, it would be a nightmare.

She wasn't due for a refresher—he'd checked her CV and knew she had a couple of months to go—but life was so much easier if they could all do the refresher in one day and with the offer of cover from the Mid-Coast team, it seemed too good to pass up.

But he'd keep an eye on her…

The unspoken words elicited a groan from deep inside his body. Metaphorically or not, he needed to see less of Emma, not more, and keeping an eye out for her?

Definitely seeing more!

It was because he was between girlfriends that he was attracted to her. It had to be that. Nothing to do with the way her eyes would twinkle at him when she laughed, or the pinkness that came into her cheeks when she was embarrassed, or the earnest way she always thanked him when he did the smallest thing for her…

This feeling of attraction was very different somehow.

Caring.

Protective.

That was it; he felt protective of her. Protective was far better than attracted…

And if he found a new girlfriend…

Wasn't there a new female assistant manager at one of the banks?

Hadn't he heard that somewhere?

Plus, if he could get Emma hooked up with someone

else, that would be even better. It would remove her from all consideration in the most positive way.

His mind began listing eligible single men—well, eligible men rather presumed their single status…

Rob Armstrong would be good. Marty had heard Rob had been in hospital recently and although he had a bit of trouble with atrial fibrillation, it responded to treatment.

But did it weaken his heart?

Ned had told him about Emma's husband—about his sudden death from cancer six years earlier. Could she handle losing another husband who might die before his time?

And just why, if he wasn't attracted to her, did the unspoken word 'husband' cause constriction in his chest?

He'd scrap Rob, but there was that new bloke on a cattle property further west—rich family sending junior to learn the ropes on one of their smaller properties.

Marty had done a bit of heli-mustering for him. He could drop in and mention the barn dance.

Better yet, he could phone the bloke, ask if they could do their practice lifts out of one of the gullies on his property. Most of his cattle were in the back country so they shouldn't be disturbed. He'd get the bloke—what *was* his name?—to act as the patient and have Emma do the lift. Clinging together at the end of the wire, who knew what chemistry might happen…?

Shane—his name was Shane.

Marty's old vehicle lacked Bluetooth so he pulled over to the side of the road and checked the contacts in his phone. Best to do it right now.

Before he forgot.

Or changed his mind…

Hiding the dread in her heart at the thought of the winch training session, Emma went in search of her father, finding him digging in the old vegetable garden out the back.

'Did you really have a good time today?' he asked shrewdly, and she smiled.

'Well, the boys did but I rather think Joss had been doing a bit of unsubtle match-making. A friend of hers, an engineer at the local council who'd been in hospital earlier in the week, also called in and it seemed a long way out of town for just a casual visit.'

'Nice bloke?' her father asked, so casually Emma had to smile.

'Nice enough,' she said, 'but that's all. Besides which, he's a patient.'

She sighed, and sat down on a corner stump that held the sleepers for the raised beds in place.

'Simon was so special, Dad, it's hard to get interested in someone else.'

Laughing blue eyes notwithstanding, she added silently.

'Do you ever think that Simon might have been so special because you had so little time together? Your marriage was still fresh and wonderful; still full of new experiences like getting to know each other, sharing tales about your lives, making plans for the future, and building dreams together.'

Emma looked at the man who'd left the work he'd loved at fifty so he could be with her during the weeks before Simon's death. Just there, in the background—ready to support her when she needed it and to hold her when the knowledge that she was losing Simon became too much to bear.

Been there, too, for the extra sadness that had followed it but she pushed that thought away, not wanting to remember her emotional and physical collapse.

He'd done some supply teaching when she'd returned to work, but he'd been there for her whenever she'd needed him, needed someone to comfort her—to just be there…

'I don't know, Dad,' she said, finally coming around

to considering his question. 'You might be right. But I do know I'll never love like that again.'

Her father kept on digging, and a cry from the house told her one of the boys was awake—and no doubt intent on waking his brother.

'I'll go. And I know I've said I'll be on deck for the kids at weekends, but I'm afraid I've got a winch training session tomorrow. We're starting early so hopefully I'll be home for lunch. Did you have anything planned?'

'Nothing I can't do with the boys. Carrie asked us all up for lunch so I'll go on ahead and you can join us if you get home in time. I've got the address in the house. Will give it to you later.'

Which kind of finished that conversation.

But was Dad right?

Had her marriage been so special—her love so strong—because it had been cut short?

Because they hadn't had time to grow niggly with each other over squeezed toothpaste tubes—although Simon had always been practically fanatical about squeezing from the bottom, whereas she just squeezed from wherever got the toothpaste out the quickest.

Hmm…

The morning dawned fearsomely bright with the promise of a still day, light winds forecast for the afternoon.

With any luck, they'd be home by afternoon, Marty decided, but would that be all good?

Carrie had phoned to invite him to lunch and insisted he come after the training session, however late that might be.

'I've asked Ned and Emma and the boys, but I guess she'll be out with you, being hauled up and down in your practising. But do come.'

Because you don't really want to be with just Ned for

too long, or because you're doing a bit of unsubtle matchmaking between Emma and me? Marty wondered.

Surely not? Carrie knew his views on commitment and marriage and she'd be the first to realise that Emma needed both.

But the sun was bright and he left all thoughts of later behind as he headed out to the base. Shane had agreed they could use his property and Marty would fly all the staff out there, then share the hovering duties with Matt.

Mark, Dave and Emma all arrived at the same time, only minutes after he'd driven in, Matt arriving close behind them.

'Okay, flight suits and helmets on, all of you,' he said, and heard Emma groan.

'Problem?' he asked, smiling at the grimace on her face.

'Only that I look like a balloon in a flight suit,' she muttered. 'One of those balloons clowns tie into funny shapes at kids' parties. It's okay for you tall people, but for us vertically challenged, it's not much fun.'

He grinned at her, but had to turn away to hide laughter when he saw what she meant. The suits did come in two sizes—small and large—but he knew they were for small and large men, not for diminutive women. With the ends of the legs and arms rolled up, and the belt cinched tight, she did kind of resemble a tied balloon.

'And why am I the only doctor here?' she demanded, obviously still grumpy.

'You're the only one with winch training. The others need to do the full course and somehow the hospital administration can't seem to find the time to send even one of the other ER doctors down to Sydney for it. It's probably why they were so happy to get you. Mac's trained, so we've used him in emergencies, particularly if the incident is over towards Wetherby.'

'Hmph,' was the reply to that, but as she'd now added her helmet and was looking like a little mushroom, Marty busied himself with the chopper.

No way was he going to tangle with a grumpy mushroom!

'We're going to a property out of town, with a good gully,' he explained when they were all ready. 'I'll land you as close as I possibly can, then you'll have to walk in—'

'Or roll in Emma's case,' Dave said, and Emma laughed and punched him lightly on the arm.

They had the makings of a really good team, Marty realised, pleased to be distracted from images of a laughing mushroom.

'I was going to say, so you can get some idea of the lie of the land. Dave and Mark can stay with me, and Mark can do the first fast response drop when you find a good spot. Matt'll sort out the order for the rest of the practice.'

Once in the air, Dave gave Matt the co-ordinates of the gully, and Marty watched as Matt tapped them into his GPS. Ten minutes' flying and he could see Shane's big four-wheel drive parked beside a dam. He landed close by, introduced his crew—Emma pulling off her helmet rather self-consciously he thought.

'Okay,' Matt said, 'let's go, kids. Dave, you act as winch man for Mark, and, Dave, you can do it for me later.'

Emma and Shane followed Matt into the gully, Shane walking beside Emma, who tried desperately to pretend this was just a nice little bushwalk. But the thought of the winch, added to her embarrassment of the unflattering flight suit, was making it difficult to follow Shane's polite conversation.

Though she did learn he kept a thousand head of cattle on his property, mostly breeding cows. The calves he sold off as weaners at about eight months for other people to fatten into steers.

At least that's what she figured from a long, slow conversation that included calving percentages, heifers kept to replace breeding cows, and the problems of getting recalcitrant cattle into cattle trucks.

Matt had signalled to the aircraft and Mark was already on his way down on the winch wire.

'You're up first,' Matt told Emma, and although she'd volunteered to go first, now the time had come she rather wished she hadn't.

Nonsense, she told herself. You've done it dozens of times—you're good at it.

Mark had reached the ground and unsnapped his harness, handing it to Emma.

'You needn't go right into the aircraft. Just strap yourself in, signal you're ready for the winch and Dave will lift you as far as the skids, then drop you back down. Hopefully you'll stay clear of the trees.'

A huge grin had accompanied the last words, and Emma glared at him as she fixed her helmet back in place and took the harness from Mark, adjusting it to her size before climbing into it and strapping in securely. She signalled to lift and up she went, reminding herself again she'd done it dozens of times, and that from what she'd seen of Marty he was an excellent pilot so would hold the aircraft in hover mode as still as he possibly could.

'Okay?' Dave called down to her as she rose above the trees.

'Just fine,' she assured him, even venturing a small wave.

He helped her onto the skids, checked she was okay, then down she went, only too happy to be back on firm ground again.

'Don't unhitch, Marty wants you to do a patient lift.'

Dave's voice came through the helmet communication and as everyone was listening she could hardly screech and yell about it.

Matt was handing Shane his helmet.

'I'm lifting Shane?' she couldn't help but yell.

Matt laughed.

'*You're* not lifting him, the winch is,' he reminded her, handing her the strop she would fit around the chest of this total stranger, before clipping him onto her harness. In this way, snapped together, they would be lifted off the ground.

Helmet to helmet, face to face, body to body.

And Shane had the hide to be grinning at her as if he was enjoying himself! It was like sharing a sleeping bag with a complete stranger, only worse because she knew all the crew would be laughing about it to themselves.

She checked all the clips and safety clasps were in place, then signalled with hand and voice that they were ready. Fortunately, their height difference—and Shane's broad shoulders—ensured she was looking at his chin, not directly into his eyes. She shifted the helmet mic away from her mouth and muttered, 'This is so embarrassing,' but she doubted he heard as they were brushing past the foliage of the trees.

In fact, he was looking all around him, as if this was a wonderful experience, put on purely so he could see this little bit of his property from a different angle.

'Lowering now.'

She sighed with relief at Mark's order. Apparently, they didn't have to go right into the aircraft for this lift either.

What she hadn't realised was that Shane's feet would touch the ground first, and he'd automatically put his hands out to steady her as she came down, holding her so close that embarrassment flooded through her.

Maybe the boys didn't need a father, she decided when

she'd unhooked, taken off her helmet, and moved a little away from the men so she could recover her composure.

Uncomfortable, that's how she'd felt.

Uneasy, too…

But surely she wouldn't feel like that with all men who touched her, no matter how platonically.

Besides which, the other part of her search for a man—what search?—had been to free up her father so he could have a life, because she knew full well he'd never leave her to cope with the boys on her own.

Considering how much he'd already given up for her, the very least she could do was *look* for a man.

And if she fell in love?

She looked around at the surrounding trees, aware deep inside herself she feared losing herself in love again, while knowing she couldn't cheat a man by not offering it.

The practice continued, Matt and Mark lifting, the helicopter landing and Matt taking over as pilot while Dave and Marty practised.

Shane had settled beside Emma on a fallen log and had been regaling her with tales of bringing the young cattle in to be ear-tagged and, in the case of the young steers, castrated.

It all sounded particularly nasty to Emma, but Shane's enthusiasm was so great she suspected he thought she was as fascinated as he was by the subject of cattle. He was telling a particularly grisly tale of having to use the tractor to haul a dead calf out of an exhausted cow when Marty called to her.

She leapt to her feet and hurried towards him, so thankful for the interruption she could have hugged him.

Until he told her why she was wanted.

'Your turn to be the patient,' he informed her, and as he was still in his harness she knew just who was going to do the lift.

Not that being held close against Marty meant any more than being held close against Shane…

Not really…

Of course it didn't.

He was tightening the strop before dropping it over her head, tightening it again under her arms, clipping them together.

'Okay?' he said, his smiling face and teasing blue eyes so close they could have kissed.

Except their helmets would have bumped together and anyway she didn't want to kiss Marty.

Definitely didn't want to kiss Marty.

Marty was the last man on earth she should consider kissing…

Would consider kissing!

'I said are you ready?'

His voice pierced the tumble of confusion in her head.

But it didn't clear the mess enough for her to speak.

She made do with a nod—bang onto his helmet—and closed her eyes because she knew he'd be laughing at her.

'Lifting now,' she heard Mark say, and kept her eyes closed because she really didn't like to look down—or even up—and for this lift she didn't have to, as Marty was in charge.

They reached the skids and Mark and Marty helped her in. Her head cleared and she hoped she wasn't blushing at the thoughts she'd had. Marty hadn't chosen her to lift, but was simply getting all the crew back on board. The winch wire and harness were already going back down for Dave, and peering out cautiously Emma realised Shane was back in his vehicle, bouncing his way across the fields towards the homestead.

Yet some wilful thread of disappointment wound its way into Emma's brain—Marty *hadn't* chosen her.

And why *should* he have?

No answer, any more than there was to the even more personal question of whether he'd felt what she'd felt, clipped so close their bodies had been touching.

Had the sudden warmth of her body transmitted itself to his?

Or had it been his that had warmed hers…?

Had he chosen Emma to lift for personal reasons?

Definitely not, he told himself as he settled back into his seat, quite happy for Matt to fly them home, as he really needed to think.

It had been a mistake, of course. He'd known that the instant he'd tightened the strop around her. Given their situations, *an*d the weird sensations he was experiencing in her vicinity, clipping her up against his body was the last thing he'd needed. It was feeling her softness despite all the harnesses and flying suits. It was catching the woman-scent of her, and seeing the clear, pale skin on her cheeks colouring slightly—with embarrassment?—and the dark, slightly curling lashes that framed her eyes.

He knew women, by some mysterious process, did curl their lashes, but he rather doubted, with the boys to be got up and fed before she'd left for the exercise, she'd have had time to curl her lashes this morning.

If she ever did.

Somehow he thought of Emma as a 'take me as you see me' kind of woman, rather than the eyelash-curling type—

But what did he know?

She was as much a mystery to him as she had been when he'd first met her.

Oh, he knew bits of her story, knew she was a loving mother to her boys, knew how much she relied on her father. Apart from that, he suspected she felt guilty about her reliance on her father, and would like to free him up in some way.

But would her father move on—and out—and leave her to cope on her own?

He doubted it.

'We're home, flyboy!' Dave said. 'Can't take the early morning start, eh?'

The rest of the crew were already climbing out, Emma in the lead and almost at the equipment shed.

He smiled to himself.

She'd want to get out of the flying suit as quickly as possible, given how much it embarrassed her. Another little insight into this woman who, for some reason, was occupying far too much of his thinking time.

And would be occupying even more of it over lunch…

'I'll see you at Carrie's,' he said, as she left the shed he was entering.

She gave him such a startled look he had to add, 'You are coming, aren't you? Carrie was furious when I told her about the winch practice and I had to promise her I'd have you back in time for lunch.'

She frowned at him.

'*You're* going to Carrie's for lunch too?' she demanded, sounding so put out he had to smile.

'Well, she *is* my sister,' he reminded her, causing the frown to turn into a scowl as she hurried away from him.

He was right, of course. Carrie *was* his sister, and he possibly had lunch with her every Sunday, but right now she wished he wasn't going. Or, failing that, that she could somehow cry off.

But she could hardly not go—it would be rude. When he turned up Carrie would know the exercise was over. Besides which, she really wanted to go, mainly so she could play with the boys and let her father catch up with his old friend.

She drove home in a daze, her mind once again such a mish-mash of thoughts it was impossible to untangle them.

Her father, the boys, a ball-kicking man, Marty—no, Marty definitely didn't fit into the slot—Carrie and her father, and what to wear to lunch, though why she was worrying about that minor detail when the rest of her life was so unsettled she had no idea.

Jeans and a top—there, that was one worry gone. She had that nice blue top she'd bought before leaving Sydney—perhaps not with jeans but her white slacks. White slacks when she'd be out with the boys? No, definitely jeans—

'We waited for you so we'd only have to take one car,' her father said as she walked up onto the veranda where the boys were explaining to the ever-patient dog that he had to stay and guard the house, although Xavier, Mr Persistent, was saying, 'But Molly and Mandy would love to see him.'

She left her father to sort out the dog and hurried through the house to shower and dress. The green top her friend Sally had given her might look better with the jeans…

Annoyed with herself for such dithering—since she'd had the boys getting dressed usually meant pulling on whatever was closest and relatively free of food stains. And even more annoyed because, although she hated to admit it, she knew it was the fact that Marty would be there that was causing the dithering.

Why he, of all men, should be affecting her the way he was, she had no idea. Could it be because she knew nothing could come of it? Not that she wanted to start regular dating, as in going out with various men. That would be bad for the boys. Wouldn't it?

But how else would she find a man?

She sighed. All she wanted was one man—one who'd

want her enough to take the boys as well—a permanent, happy-to-be-with-her man, a friend to share her life, a father for her boys, but definitely not a commitment-phobe.

The green top made her eyes look green—a greyish green for sure, but better than dull grey…

CHAPTER FIVE

LUNCH WITH CARRIE turned out to be a party—a small party admittedly but more than a casual lunch. Mac and Izzy were there—well, like Marty, they were family—and another couple who were friends of Carrie's from her work in the local government office.

And had the tall, bespectacled man Carrie introduced as Neil been asked especially for her—Emma—or had he kind of latched onto her because he didn't know anyone else?

'Neil's the local agronomist, and he's not been in town very long,' Carrie had said by way of a succinct introduction, and although Emma's mind connected the job description with agriculture, she really had no idea what he might do.

The polite thing to do was ask, and as Molly and Mandy had taken her boys off to play in the garden, and she and Neil were kind of in a space of their own, she *did* ask and was soon being treated to a lesson on crop yields and safer farrowing methods for free-range pigs.

She looked desperately around for someone to rescue her, but her father was talking to Carrie's friends, while Mac had taken charge of the barbecue and Izzy was helping Carrie produce bowls of salad and plates of meat. Which left Marty, who was actually watching her, and must have been aware of her predicament as he was grinning with malicious delight.

She threw a murderous frown in his direction and suggested to Neil that they look at the garden, knowing how easily her boys could create a diversion.

Neil seemed a trifle taken aback, for he was in the middle of an extremely complicated—to Emma—story about a horse that had been cast in its stall. But he followed her—albeit reluctantly—out to the garden, where Marty had now materialised and was kicking a football with the boys—the two girls acting as goalies for the hectic game.

A side kick from Marty brought the ball to Neil's feet and although even Emma's instinctive reaction would have been to kick it back, there it sat.

'Kick it here,' Hamish shouted.

'No, here,' Xavier insisted.

But in the end it was Emma who kicked it, not to either of the boys but to Molly—or perhaps Mandy…

Yet the incident stayed with Emma for the rest of the day. At lunch she'd managed to sit down between her father and Izzy, Neil opposite her at the table, explaining something about mung beans to Mac, who was obviously a lot better at looking interested than Emma had been.

But Neil, although she had no doubt he'd been invited to meet her, wasn't the subject of her preoccupation. No, it was Marty kicking the football right to Neil's feet that had disturbed her.

Not because Neil hadn't kicked it back—she'd been talking to him long enough to realise he probably hadn't even noticed it—but that Marty had tested him in that way.

Because it *had* been a test.

Yet try as she might, she couldn't recall ever mentioning to Marty her vague idea that a ball-kicking man might be good to have around for the boys' sake…

Had he divined it?

Read her thoughts?

Had she told Joss and it had become hospital gossip?

She had no idea, yet she knew as well as she knew her own name that Marty had kicked that ball as a test…

Neil claimed her when lunch was finished, and, desperate for a conversation that didn't involve farm animals or crops, she asked if he was going to the barn dance the following weekend.

'Oh, yes,' he said, adding with obvious pride, 'I'm going to be the auctioneer. I did a bit of cattle auctioneering when I was in Queensland—mostly Brahman crossbreeds where I was stationed. They're big beasts and tick-free, which is essential in those parts.'

Emma hid an inner sigh as she just knew she'd soon know more about Brahman crossbreeds than she'd ever needed to know.

But Neil surprised her.

'If you're going, maybe you can act as my assistant,' he suggested, beaming at her as if he'd just conferred a great honour on her. 'Just passing me the slips with the information about the animals to be auctioned and such.'

'Wouldn't you have them in a pile on the lectern?' she said, possibly a little snappishly as the thought of spending the entire evening discussing various aspects of agriculture filled her with horror.

But Neil was undaunted.

'You're right, but perhaps you could spot the bidders. You know, let me know who won each lot.'

'You need someone who knows the locals for that job,' a voice behind Emma said, and the little hairs standing up on the back of her neck told her as much as the voice did.

Marty.

Relief at being rescued made her turn to him, smiling far too brightly.

'You sound as if you've had practice,' she said, moving a little closer to him.

Unconsciously hoping Neil might see them as a couple?

She could feel embarrassment colouring her cheeks that she'd even *thought* such a thing.

And as for using Marty, of all people, as a cover?

Hardly fair…

'Emma?'

Lost in thought, she'd missed whatever conversation had been going on between Neil and Marty, but apparently one of them had included her in it.

'Sorry,' she said. 'I was distracted by the boys.'

Which she now was, as Hamish was attempting to hold the ball behind his back—not easy for someone only three feet tall—while Xavier howled and dashed around him, this way and that, as Hamish twisted and turned.

'Got to halt the war,' she said over her shoulder as she moved to separate the two, who were now rolling on the ground, wrestling with each other, the ball forgotten.

Molly and Mandy arrived at the same time she did, but she smiled at the girls as she separated the boys.

'You girls deserve a break,' she said, holding the boys close to her. 'While you two rascals can walk around the garden with me. I'm sure if we look hard we can find a caterpillar or a snail or maybe even a grasshopper.'

They prepared to race off but she was quicker, grabbing one hand of each of them to keep them anchored to the spot.

'We need to walk quietly so we don't frighten the caterpillar.'

So, with the boys now tiptoeing, they set off to search Carrie's generous-sized garden, squatting down now and then to lift a leaf or check a low-lying branch.

'You left me listening to that man talk about sow farrowing!'

The note of reproach in Marty's voice as he came up behind them made Emma smile, but as the boys had also heard his voice and were greeting him with a chorus of 'Marty' and demands that he help them find a caterpillar, she had no choice but to let him join the hunt.

They were at the far end of the garden when Carrie called, 'Ice cream for whoever wants it,' and the boys shot off.

Emma looked at the man who could not only kick footballs but had the endless patience required for caterpillar searches.

'You're so good with children,' she said suddenly, 'so why the no-commitment rule? Why not marry and have some of your own?'

She looked into his eyes, no longer laughing but filled with a great sadness.

And for a moment she thought he might speak—might tell her what had caused it, what held him back.

But he shook his head, then touched her gently on the shoulder.

'It's just something I decided a long time ago,' he said quietly. 'Something to do with history repeating itself, which we see so often in life.'

She should let it go at that, she knew, but his words were so bleak and she could feel such pain emanating from his body.

She put her hand on his where it still rested on her shoulder.

'How long ago?' she asked, and he gave a huff of laughter that held no mirth, although his eyes looked better now—almost smiling at her.

'Too long, lovely lady,' he said, then he bent his head and kissed her, ever so lightly, on the lips, running his hand through her hair as he added, 'Way too long to ever change my mind about it.'

And he walked away.

Emma watched him go, one hand pressed against the lips he'd just kissed, her body tingling from that, oh, so light touch.

He's not for you, her head said bluntly, while her heart grew heavy in her chest, and a longing she barely understood filled her body.

But her head was right—hadn't Marty said as much?

He was not for her…

Hell's teeth! What had he been thinking, kissing Emma?

Though it hadn't been a real kiss—

Then why had his toes curled?

Okay, so no more kisses, not even unreal ones…

He headed for his car. He'd call Carrie later and apologise for leaving without saying goodbye to everyone. At least they were all out the back in the barbecue area, eating ice cream.

Except Emma.

But when he turned his head, he saw that she, too, had moved, so hopefully no one would see or even notice his strategic retreat.

Except Izzy, of course. It was nearly dinner time and he'd just returned from the base where he'd been doing some work on his own chopper—something that up until today had always soothed him—when Izzy phoned.

'You left very suddenly,' she said.

'Stating the obvious, Iz?'

'Well, you did! It's Emma, isn't it? Emma and that stubborn streak of yours about commitment. Honestly, Marty, of all of us, I thought you were the most sensible—the most stable—and you were Hallie and Pop's kid from the time you were five or six, so *they* were your parents, *that* house was your home—your life.'

'Leave it, Iz,' he said quietly, and she did because they had all *always* respected each other's boundaries.

'So tell me about That Man,' she said, and he knew she was talking about Neil.

'Got caught by him, did you?' he teased. 'I can't think why Carrie invited him.'

'For Emma, of course,' Izzy replied, 'although Carrie mustn't have known him well—just that he wasn't downright ugly and was single. She couldn't possibly have had a conversation with him. He spent half an hour telling me how young boars sometimes have difficulty mating and how a boar's penis is shaped like a corkscrew.'

Marty roared with laughter, only stopping when Izzy said frostily, 'It's all very well for you to laugh. I couldn't get away from him. Mac was there, pretending to clean the barbecue, but he was secretly enjoying it so much he didn't want to rescue me.'

Marty apologised but Izzy was having none of it.

'You're still smiling, I can hear it in your voice. How is Emma? Did she get over being stranded on the beach? Is she enjoying Braxton? Those boys of hers are a handful, but Ned seems to be able to handle them.'

'He does, but I suspect it's starting to worry Emma that he gives so much of his time—his life really—to her and the boys. I'm sure that's why Carrie asked Neil to the party. I think she'd like to get Emma married off.'

'For her sake or for Emma's?' Izzy asked, and Marty laughed again.

'You don't miss much, do you?'

But he was more relaxed now. Talking about Carrie and Ned and a possible romance there had got Izzy off the subject of his commitment to remain single.

Izzy was the most perceptive of his siblings—probably because she lived close by and saw more of him than the others did.

But for all that Pop had been the father figure he had followed and still adored, his memories of the fear and rage he'd felt towards his birth father were still too strong, too vivid, to ever be forgotten.

And that man's genes were embedded deep within him. So he had no intention of ever putting them to the test…

Emma collected her tired and grubby boys after the ice creams had been consumed, telling her father to stay on and enjoy himself.

'The boys and I both need a rest,' she added, as Carrie helped out by insisting Ned stay on.

But although the boys, once bathed and free of sticky ice cream, went peacefully off to sleep, and she tried to rest, she remained awake, staring at the ceiling, her mind—and other bits of her body—remembering the kiss.

Not that it was a real kiss, she kept reminding herself, but if it wasn't real, why did even remembering it make her lips tingle?

But the no-commitment thing had been laid out, made plain to her in no uncertain terms. So tingly lips were about all she'd ever get from Marty—tingly lips and friendship—she was pretty sure that was still intact.

She sighed, and because the ceiling wasn't giving her any answers she gave up pretending to rest and went into the kitchen. She'd have a baking afternoon, fill the biscuit tins, maybe make some meals that could be frozen for nights when she didn't feel like cooking.

Not that she cooked that often in the evening, but if she was going to push her father further into whatever social life Braxton held for men his age, then she'd have to get used to it. Carrie's friends had mentioned a bridge club and her father had always loved a game of bridge.

He arrived home as she finished washing the pots and pans that didn't fit in the dishwasher.

He picked up a tea-towel, but she took it out of his hands.

'There's football on the telly, go and watch it. We came to Braxton for a change and I've started my changing with a new job and new friends at work, so it's time you started yours. I'm going to take over more responsibility for the boys and if I'm not here, I'll get the girls, or one of them, to babysit. For a start, you should join the bridge club.'

He took the tea-towel out of her hands and lifted a wet pot.

'I've already said I'd go to the quiz night at the bottom pub on Tuesday night,' he told her, smiling as she looked surprised. 'And spoken to Molly and Mandy in case you're held up at work.'

'Well!' Emma said. 'Good for you!'

And she reached out and hugged him, the pot caught between them, tears pricking at her eyes.

'I can never thank you enough for all you've done for me and the boys, and for just being there for me through so much.'

He finished his task, slipped the pot into a drawer, then turned to face her, reaching out to touch her cheek.

'I wouldn't have been happy not being there,' he said quietly. 'Hadn't you ever realised that?'

She shook her head, a couple of tears escaping now. Swiping them away, she smiled at him.

'I don't suppose I had, but now we're living here, and the boys are nearly ready for kindy, it's time you had a life of your own.'

He smiled back and kissed her on the forehead.

'I will,' he promised, 'but for now get out of my kitchen. You're probably putting things back in the wrong places. I thought after the big lunch we might just have cheese on toast for dinner.'

'Sounds great! And I'll cook it. Cheese on toast is something of a specialty for me.'

A shuffling noise from the direction of the boys' bedroom told her at least one of them was awake. And if one was, the other soon would be. Hoping to spend some alone time with whoever was awake, she hurried in, grabbing Xavier as he prepared to climb onto Hamish's cot and bounce him awake.

'How about you and I do some painting on the veranda?' she said quietly, carrying him out of the room before he had time to make a noise.

'Finger-painting?' Xavier asked hopefully, and after shaking away the knowledge of just how much mess that would entail, she agreed.

It was a quieter week in A and E, and with Emma working an early shift she was able to be home with the boys by three. Most days she would then shoo her father out of the house, insisting he do something for himself.

'I'm playing snooker on Thursday night,' he protested.

'Not enough,' she told him. 'Go to the library. I know you take the boys there for story-time on Tuesdays but that's hardly a peaceful, fruitful visit. You used to love poking around in libraries, and now you're back in Braxton, you can read up on the history of the place. I doubt you had much interest in it when you were young.'

He smiled at her.

'Actually, I did. I must have been a complete nerd because the library was my favourite place and it has always had a great local history section. I'll see what I can find out about the history of this house because it must have been one of the first built here in town.'

The briskness in her father's footsteps as he crossed the veranda told her he was pleased to be free, and she smiled to herself.

Maybe if she could prove to him that she could juggle work and the boys by herself, she wouldn't have to worry about finding a man. She was making playdough while she considered this and telling herself that of course it would work.

After all, many single women coped with work and a family—coped very well in most cases. She just had to show her father that she could, too.

And the heavy feeling in her heart as she thought about these things was to do with the loss of the man she'd had—nothing at all to do with a vague idea that maybe she, too, could do with a man around the place.

Footsteps across the veranda—her father returning so quickly?

'Anyone home?'

Marty!

'In the kitchen,' she called back, but the comings and goings had woken the boys from their afternoon sleep, and her only reaction to Marty's 'I'll get them,' was one of relief.

At least she could wash the sticky dough off her hands, and probably her face, before he came in.

But when he did come in, a beaming boy on each arm, the dog at his heels, her heart stood still.

Maybe she did need a man, a voice in her head whispered. A man to make a family—father, mother, children, and a dog—surely the picture-perfect family?

So, a man—

Just not this one, another voice pointed out. He wasn't available.

Somehow they were all around the table, Marty making a pot of tea while Emma rolled the dough in flour to lessen the stickiness and divided it into two pieces.

'It's green,' Hamish pointed out, quite unnecessarily.

'Very green,' this from Marty as he put the teapot on its stand in the middle of the table.

'We can make frogs,' Xavier said, sheer delight in his voice and face.

'Out on the veranda, and not until you've had your snack,' Emma told them, getting up and washing her hands again—and, no, green food colouring didn't come off with soap and water.

She found biscuits and sultanas for the boys, poured each of them a glass of milk, then sat down to have a cup of tea, Marty already having found mugs, small plates and the biscuit tin.

Yes, maybe a husband would come in handy sometimes. But no more than that. She could easily manage without one.

'Your hands are green,' Hamish told her.

'Really?' she teased. 'I thought they were purple.'

'No, definitely green,' her more serious son, Xavier, assured her.

But the lure of green hands ended the boys' conversation as they scoffed down their snacks, drank their milk and headed, green balls in hand, for their play table on the veranda.

'Too much food colouring?' Marty asked.

He was seated opposite her, across a wide, old, kitchen table that really wasn't wide enough. But she had other distractions right now.

'Dad does all this stuff so easily,' she said, sighing and running her green fingers through her hair to push it off her face. 'I do so want to set him free—to get him out and about, and leading a life of his own—but he worries about how I'll cope. And then there's the boys—growing up without a father, especially when they reach puberty, and start asking questions. I know heaps of kids do grow up without a father, but what if they feel cheated later?'

She paused, shaking away the thoughts tumbling through her head, then looked across the table at Marty.

'I really do need a man,' she said, the words bursting from her lips before she realised just how desperate they sounded.

Not to mention pathetic!

Although who better to tell than a man who wasn't interested in her himself?

Wouldn't it be handy to have his opinion on the subject?

'I know I should be able to cope on my own, and I'm sure I could, but it's making Dad see it.'

Marty was sipping his tea, but looked interested enough for her to continue.

'If I had a man, then Dad would feel it was okay to get on with his own life because he wouldn't be leaving me alone. I'd thought of it—not hard, but there'd been a tiny seed of an idea—back there in Sydney. I'd been thinking it might be good for the kids to have a father. It's only since I've been up here and seen Dad with people of his own age that I realise how selfish I've been not to have let him go before now.'

'I don't think it was a matter of you letting him go, but more he wouldn't have left you on your own,' Marty pointed out.

'That's the problem.'

She was about to say more but noises from the veranda had Emma on her feet.

Green froth around the dog's mouth explained what had happened, and as Xavier was wailing, it was his play-dough the 'puppy' had eaten.

Emma divided the remaining dough, ignoring Hamish's protests, and they settled down again, but she knew the game was losing their attention and was relieved when Marty appeared with their two cups of tea.

'If we sit here, we can watch them,' he said, hitching a cane table closer with his foot. He set down the tea and brought over two chairs.

Emma gave a huff of laughter and half smiled as she said, 'You can see why having a man around would be easier.'

Marty looked at the woman who was causing chaos in his mind and body, agreeing with the idea she needed a man but for different reasons. If she was married he'd no longer be interested in her—he hoped—because he'd always avoided the unnecessary complications of dating a married woman. As far as he was concerned, it just wasn't done.

But all her talk of having a man around didn't seem to be making her happy. In fact—

'You said that as if, while it might be easier as far as managing the boys goes, *and* freeing up your father, you'd see it as a nuisance—a penance of some kind. Something you'd be doing solely for your father and the boys and not for yourself.'

She frowned at him over her teacup.

'Would it matter why I wanted him?' she asked.

'It might to him,' Marty pointed out, and she frowned again.

'Why?'

He studied her for a moment.

'Well, from all you've told me, you could hire a housekeeper. It's a big house, so she could live in, be around for you and the boys, satisfy your father that there was someone there for you.'

'But…' She shook her head as if trying to dislodge the words she needed. Tried again. 'But she wouldn't be a *father* to the boys.'

'You haven't thought this through at all, have you?' Marty asked, more than slightly bemused by the situation. 'If this unknown man is to be a father to your boys, he'd have to be your husband. You should be thinking of a man for yourself, not the boys. Thinking of what *you* want first.'

He saw the colour creep into her cheeks.

Embarrassment or anger?

'I do know I'd have obligations,' she said, obviously embarrassed now. 'I'm not completely stupid. I'd probably even enjoy the kind of closeness sex brings.'

She'd dropped her voice before mentioning the 's' word but the boys were further down the veranda now, wrestling with the dog.

'And love?'

'What about it?' she demanded, looking directly into his eyes, as if daring him to continue the conversation.

He shrugged, sure she knew exactly what he meant.

They sat in silence for a minute, then she reached out and touched his hand where it lay on the table by his teacup.

'I'm sorry, it's just the love thing, the risk of it. I don't know if I could do it again. But I shouldn't argue with you of all people. You're the only real friend I feel I've made so far in Braxton.'

Marty's hand burned from the touch but he knew he was an inch away from quicksand.

'It's what I hang around for,' he said, hoping he sounded far more disinterested than he felt. 'Just someone to be snapped at, and thank you for the friend part. Friends are precious.'

Unsure he could maintain his air of detachment, he stood up, collected both cups, and walked through to the kitchen.

'I'd better be going,' he said as he returned to the veranda. 'Only called in to say I'm happy to drive you and Ned to the barn dance on Saturday night. I'll come by at about six-thirty. It's a twenty-minute drive out along the

Wetherby road. Wear jeans, check shirts, straw-in-mouth kind of gear.'

He paused before adding, 'Oh, and we all bring our own picnic supper. Izzy and Mac will be joining our group, so Carrie will probably arrange who brings what. She'll be in touch.'

'We'll be ready,' Emma said, but all emotion had been wiped from her voice, and her face was pale and still.

Had he hurt her with his talk of love? The thought made him uncomfortable in a way he didn't want to think about.

Deep down uncomfortable…

A whole new emotional discomfort he'd never experienced before…

Love?

No way!

'Then I'm off,' he said, and called out goodbye to the boys.

That gave her time to get to her feet and come to the top of the steps.

'You're right, friends are precious,' she said, taking his hand and holding it as she reached up to kiss his cheek. 'Thank you for being mine.'

He walked down the steps, his mind keeping pace with his feet. I will not touch my cheek. I am not sixteen, and bowled over by a first kiss. And I won't turn around, for all I know, she's watching me.

He lasted until he reached the gate, when he did turn, and wave, and if his hand accidentally touched his cheek as it dropped back into place, well, that wasn't all that adolescent!

CHAPTER SIX

SATURDAY FINALLY ARRIVED, and although Emma was secretly dreading this first social event of her life in Braxton, she was excited as well.

And, no, she told herself firmly, it had nothing to do with seeing Marty again.

He'd been conspicuous by his absence at the hospital all week, although she knew two new patients in the post-op ward had been brought in from outlying properties by the rescue helicopter.

She'd even looked out for him in case he came to visit the new patients, then chided herself for caring.

But as she made a large salad on Saturday afternoon, and phoned Carrie to ask if she needed to bring plates and cutlery, her excitement grew.

Because she'd be seeing Marty?

She blanked the thought, replaced it with the knowledge that her father would enjoy meeting up with old school friends again, and maybe get involved in more local activities. Marty had been right, she could get a housekeeper, even part time. That would free up her father to pursue a new life.

They'd work out a schedule to give him more free time.

She was in her bedroom, looking through her wardrobe for something that would pass for a country shirt, when her father called from the hall.

'Ta-da!' he said, grinning from ear to ear and looking utterly ridiculous in a too-small hat with pigtails hanging from it.

'I don't think it's a back to childhood party,' she told him when she stopped laughing.

He took it off and handed it to her.

'It's for you. I found it in a junk shop and I've wiped it out with antiseptic, though I doubt, from the look of it, it's ever been worn. Do try it on.'

She pulled the hat onto her head, arranged the pigtails so they fell across her ears, and bowed to her delighted father.

'Great!' he said, and he went off to get dressed himself, although when she saw him, he didn't look much different to his usual self in tan chinos and, yes, a checked shirt, but he had tied a bandana around his neck and then produced from behind his back a hat with corks dangling from it.

'We'll make the perfect Aussie couple,' he told her, offering her his arm and sweeping her into a wild dance down the hall.

'Hey!' she finally said. 'I've got to finish getting ready. You could put the salad in the big basket and pack some cold drinks into a cool box. Marty will be here before we know it.'

And he was, coming up the front steps to tell them he already had Carrie in the car, and ask if they were ready.

He roared with laughter at Emma's hat.

'That's priceless!' he finally said. 'You'll fit right in.'

She said goodnight to the boys, and reminded the babysitters to call her cellphone if there were any problems, then followed the men to the car.

The drive took them through some of the burnt-out bushland, legacy of the fire, and although it made Emma feel a little sad, her driver, the eternal optimist, pointed out green shoots already sprouting from some of the trees and bushes.

'The Aborigines used fire to regenerate their land,' her father said. 'They did it carefully, in patches, so there was always fresh food for the animals and fresh seeds and nuts for themselves.'

The road wound through the mountains, then opened out onto green farmland.

'We turn off here—the sanctuary is just down this lane,' Carrie explained.

And soon they began to see the animals, horses so old they moved slowly but were probably still loved by the families who could no longer keep them.

Goats and donkeys abounded, and Emma was delighted.

'Do they allow visitors? Could I bring the boys out here?' she asked, and Carrie laughed.

'Of course you can. It's how they make most of their money,' she explained. 'You pay a small admission charge and there are set visiting hours, but with busloads of school kids coming, as well as families at weekends, they get a fair bit. The barn dance and auction top it off, and usually that money goes towards building repairs.'

'What's the auction about?' Emma asked. 'What gets auctioned?'

'The animals,' Marty said, breaking a silence that had seemed to be too long.

'You can bid for any of the animals, and whatever you bid goes to that animal for the year. I think Mac got the three-legged goat his first year here.'

'Poor Mac,' Carrie said. 'He hardly knew what had hit him when he was thrust into this family.'

'Hardly knew what had hit him when he met Izzy,' Marty pointed out, and Carrie agreed that their romance *had* been something special.

But ahead Emma could see lights, and hear music, and soon the lights showed her the largest barn she'd ever seen.

'It looks like more like a three-storey building,' she said, and the others agreed.

'Bloke who built it had a combine harvester and several other large farm machines. He contracted out to farmers who didn't want to keep expensive machinery sitting around for most of the year when there was someone who would come in and do the job. He knew Meg, who runs the centre, and knew her premises were growing too small, so he left the place to her in his will—the whole property.'

'It was a wonderful gift,' Ned said, looking around, while Emma's attention was on the barn and the people gathered about a bar just inside the doorway.

She was sure she'd spotted Neil and was wondering how she could get through a whole evening without being caught up with him when Carrie said, 'Oh, no, it's Neil. Emma, I do apologise for inviting him for lunch, but I'd only spoken a few words to him in the corridors at work and thought he'd be okay.'

'I'll keep him occupied,' Ned offered. 'Maybe not all night because I'm here to dance, but I'll keep watch and if he nabbles you, Em, I'll steer him away. I'm actually quite interested in the agricultural produce of the area. Things have changed a lot since I grew up here.'

It didn't take long for Emma to realise she was really enjoying herself. Many of the staff from the hospital were there, and she was whirled from one country dance to another.

To her delight, she saw her father was also enjoying himself, sometimes dancing but more often deep in conversation with men and women his age—no doubt old school friends.

'This was the best decision we've ever made, me and Dad,' she said to Marty when he appeared from nowhere and claimed a dance. 'Just look at him, he's having the time of his life.'

Marty looked over to where Ned was engaged in a spirited dance with Gladys from the milk bar, talking and laughing at the same time.

'How he's got enough breath to talk beats me,' Emma said.

'Does it matter?' Marty asked, teasing blue eyes looking down into hers.

'Of course not,' Emma managed, although she knew her face had grown hot and her whole body had reacted to that look.

Marty pulled her closer.

'I'd like to whisk you away behind a deserted hay bale,' he murmured in her ear.

Emma recovered enough sense to retort, 'If you could find one—deserted, I mean.'

But her mind wasn't completely on the conversation. Some distance away, sitting quietly on a rug-covered straw bale, Izzy was looking far from well.

Emma looked around, and saw Mac dancing on the other side of the barn.

'Let's go see Izzy,' she said to Marty, who'd been slowly drawing her closer and closer in his arms.

He began to protest, but Emma was already moving away, wending her way through the revellers to where she'd seen Izzy.

'Are you okay?' she asked, when she reached the flushed and slightly shaky woman.

'I think so,' Izzy replied. 'Just suddenly didn't feel well. I probably shouldn't have been rollicking around so much on the dance floor and it's made me a bit dizzy, as if my head's still whirling.'

But Emma was already checking her out. Some swelling of the feet and ankles—fairly normal in pregnancy—

but as she took Izzy's hand she saw it was also swollen, her wedding ring biting into her finger.

She slid her fingers up the swollen wrist to feel for a pulse—definitely high—and turned to Marty, who had appeared beside her.

'Get Mac to come over, take his car keys and get his car as close to the door as you can, then ask Dad if he'll drive your car and Carrie back to Braxton. It could be pre-eclampsia and we should get Izzy to the hospital in Braxton as soon as possible just in case.'

Memories threatened. Memories of shock and fear, but she pushed them away. Izzy needed her to be at her best.

To Izzy she said, 'You'll be fine. It's a precaution, but you have enough medical experience to know if it *is* pre-eclampsia you need treatment right away.'

She hoped she sounded calm and efficient but inwardly she was a mess. Had she made a promise she couldn't keep; would all be well for Izzy and the baby? And what had she been doing, fiddling around with a pigtail hat when she should have been putting an emergency bag of drugs in the car?

Mac arrived, his face tense and strained, although he was so gentle and loving with Izzy, Emma felt like crying.

'Possible pre-eclampsia?' he asked, touching his wife's face where fluid had collected.

Emma nodded.

'I'll get Marty to drive your car, you can sit in the front, and I'll sit in the back with Izzy and do whatever I can to make her comfortable.'

'I could do that,' Mac protested. 'I'm a doctor, too.'

'And she's your wife—that's enough pressure for you. And Marty knows these roads better than anyone, but you'll still have your car in Braxton when you need it.'

As she could see Marty beckoning from the door, she got the party moving, Mac lifting Izzy into his arms as though she were a featherweight and striding urgently towards the door.

The music had stopped and people were stepping back—leaving room for him to carry her swiftly to the car. Ned caught up with Emma.

'You okay?' he asked, and she smiled and gave him a quick hug, aware he, too, was remembering what had happened to her.

'Right as rain,' she told him. 'You'll take Marty's car back to town—and Carrie?'

Her father nodded.

'Get going, and good luck,' he said, pacing beside her as far as the door.

Mac had settled Izzy into the rear seat, her feet up and a pillow collected from somewhere placed behind her back.

Emma scrambled into the footwell, where she would be close to Izzy and able to keep an eye on her condition. She had to focus on Izzy now—to the exclusion of all else. The past was the past.

'Let's go,' she said, and Marty needed no second telling.

The drive, along winding mountain roads, seemed endless, although they must have made it to the hospital in record time. Marty had given Mac the relevant phone numbers to call so by the time they pulled up at the emergency doors, they had not only a trolley and staff waiting but Izzy's obstetrician.

Emma hung back as Izzy was wheeled away, to be examined, treated, and have decisions made about her condition and the safety of both her and the baby. There were so many variables—and so many risks—connected to the condition, Emma found herself shivering as she followed the parade into the ED.

'I think I should go and get Nikki.'

Just when Marty had caught up with her, Emma wasn't

sure, but when he materialised beside her she wasn't altogether surprised. He made a habit of it, the materialising thing…

She turned to him and nodded.

'You're right, I think she'd like to be here. You'll be, what, a couple of hours? I can explain to Mac—'

'Couple of hours be damned, I'll fly over. I'll phone Hallie to let her know I'm coming and what's going on, and she'll track Nikki down.'

He paused, then smiled—the kind of smile that Emma wished had been for her.

'Come to think of it, Hallie will want to be here too, and I think Izzy might need her.'

He really was a special person, Emma thought as Marty dashed off. Always thinking of others, thinking ahead then working out the best way he could help.

As special as Simon?

The thought was so startling she stopped in her tracks, shook off her straying thoughts and walked swiftly into the emergency room, where Izzy was being examined.

Except she wasn't there. Mac met her at the door.

'They've decided to deliver the baby, she's been wheeled up to theatre for a Caesar,' he said, his voice tight with strain. 'She's only thirty-one weeks, but the foetal heartbeat isn't that great. She's had anticonvulsant medication and steroids to help the baby's lungs develop more quickly, but her obstetrician doesn't want to wait.'

'Thirty-one weeks? Braxton PICU won't be able to keep the baby. He or she—'

'He,' Mac put in. 'We only decided at the last scan that we wanted to know, and, yes, I'd been thinking the same thing. Where will they send them?'

'I haven't been here long enough to know,' Emma told him. 'But I'd say Retford. It's the major hospital in the region and as it's attached to the regional university I would think they'd have a top-class PICU.'

Mac gave a huff of laughter.

'I actually know that, having sent a baby there myself. Shows the state I'm in.'

'As does the fact you're standing here chatting with me. I know they'll have to prep Izzy for the op, but shouldn't you be up in Theatre, waiting for her?'

Mac's face paled.

'Of course,' he said, his voice so hoarse Emma could read the fear he felt for his wife.

'They'll both be fine, so go,' she said to him, giving him a little push in the direction of the theatre.

Should she follow?

Could she follow?

She'd been battling to keep focussed from the moment she'd crossed the barn to sit beside Izzy, battling to keep away the memories that were threatening to flood her brain and render her totally useless. Thinking about Marty to distract herself?

But they could no longer be pushed back, and as she walked along the corridor towards the theatre she remembered being wheeled in, still numb from Simon's death, not really aware of anything that was happening around her, let alone within her body.

She turned, seeking privacy in the ER tea-room, quiet at night with only a skeleton staff on duty. She fiddled with the kettle so if anyone came in she'd have her back to them and at least *look* busy.

And now she let the memories flood in. The mad dash to the hospital, pre-eclampsia—the dreaded word—being muttered somewhere outside the fog that was in her head.

Decisions being made by experts because this had been one shock too many for her. Bed rest not helping, and a Caesar the only option.

But her baby, Simon's baby, hadn't lived and now the tears she hadn't been able to shed then because Simon's death had left her empty—now those tears, the tears for her baby, rolled down her cheeks.

'Has something happened? Izzy? The baby?'

Once again Marty was there, behind her this time. She swiped away the tears, aware she must have been staring at the kettle for at least an hour.

Probably longer…

'They're fine, as far as I know,' she said, turning to find not only Marty in the room but a teenager Emma assumed must be Nikki, with Hallie close behind her.

'We should hear soon,' she told them. 'I was thinking tea if anyone wants one. You might like coffee, Marty. Or is Matt on duty? Because the baby will be too premmie for Braxton so they'll all have to be flown to Retford.'

He didn't answer, too busy studying her face, so many questions in his eyes she had to turn away and wipe her face again before greeting Hallie.

'And you must be Nikki,' she said, holding out her hand to the teenager. 'I've got some clothes of yours I should have returned earlier.'

'Keep them,' Nikki told her. 'Mum bought me new ones anyway.'

She spoke brightly but her face clouded over at the thought of her mother.

'How is she? Will she be all right? And the baby?'

'Everyone will be fine,' Hallie announced, and the certainty in her voice not only made Emma smile but also eased some of the hard edges of the grief that had struck her so suddenly.

'I'll organise the chopper to take them both to Retford,' Marty said. 'We'll take a PICU nurse and can take Mac too.'

He looked at Hallie.

'Good idea,' she said. 'We'll wait until we've seen Izzy then Nikki and I can take Mac's car to Carrie's, spend the night there, and drive down to Retford in the morning.'

Emma shook her head.

'You're some organised family, aren't you?' she said, and Hallie laughed.

'We had to be,' she said. 'We had eight kids with us at one stage. How many with your lot, Marty?'

He counted them off on his fingers.

'Steve, me, Izzy, Lila and Liane—that's five, hardly any at all.'

'And more trouble than all the rest put together,' Hallie said sternly, but Emma saw the twinkle in her eyes and wondered if that group—her last lot of foster children—had maybe been her favourite.

Marty knew he had to leave, but the sadness and the sheen of tears he'd caught on Emma's face made him want to comfort her—to hold her, even, though that could never be. If ever there was a woman who needed commitment it was Emma.

'Let's get up to Theatre. Both mother and baby should be cleaned up by now and we can all say hello before I have to fly them away.'

He led the way, hoping Emma would follow and he'd have a chance to speak to her while Hallie and Nikki spent a few moments with Izzy.

But it was not to be.

When they all trooped into the small recovery room where Izzy lay pale but smiling, and Mac was hovering protectively over a humidicrib inhabited by quite a robust-looking baby, Emma was nowhere to be seen.

He left the family there, knowing he had work to do, knowing too that a PICU nurse would be accompanying them on the flight so there'd be no need for Emma.

Yet wanting to see her, find out about that awful sadness he'd read in her lovely eyes…

It's none of your business, he reminded himself as he headed for the base. An ambulance would bring his passengers out there, and he had to be fully prepared for the flight.

Extra fully prepared for he'd be carrying precious cargo—family cargo.

Family…

Emma had watched them all go off to see Izzy and the baby but she couldn't follow, because, although her tears no longer flowed, she didn't want the misery she'd been feeling to taint the delight of a new birth—even if it was a premmie one.

So she walked home, and even found a smile when she saw the light burning at the top of the front steps, welcoming her back.

Home.

She nodded to herself, aware that this old house, with its high ceilings and large airy rooms, the warm family kitchen and the untidy garden with its mango trees, had become just that—a home.

And that being the case, she decided as she climbed the steps, she had to stop thinking about Marty Graham. He wasn't for her, they both knew that, so if she wanted a man in her life—for the boys' sake *and* to free up her father—she'd have to start sifting through the available men in the town.

She walked inside, checked the boys in their beds, and read the note her father had left on the kitchen table. Carrie had driven him home and taken Molly and Mandy home with her. Boys quiet all night, had fun at the barn dance, talk in the morning.

It was a comforting note, but the fact that he'd had fun

then had had to come home to mind her children, drove home the need for her to find a man—or a housekeeper.

A housekeeper who could kick a football maybe?

She made a cup of tea, having failed to make one at the hospital, and took it with her to the front veranda, where she settled on the top step to look out at the sleeping town.

So far she'd met three available men, the meetings engineered by helpful friends or colleagues. There was the engineer, Rob Armstrong—a nice enough guy but she kind of suspected he might be holding a torch for Joss, and although Joss was happily married, he'd shown absolutely no interest in her, Emma.

Neil didn't need consideration, although maybe she was being a trifle unkind. There'd be some woman somewhere out there who'd love to know how many tons per acre a good mung bean crop should produce, he just wasn't Emma's cup of tea.

She drained the real cup of tea and sighed. She was fairly certain they'd done their winch practice on Shane's property so Marty could engineer a meeting between her and Shane.

Shane who?

Had she ever heard his surname?

Not that it mattered, just thinking of their possible wedding photos—hers and Shane's—with her looking like a midget beside him, was enough for her to know he wasn't worth pursuing.

This was ridiculous. None of these men had shown the slightest interest in her, and even if one had, how fair would it be to use any one of them as a distraction from Marty?

Marty, whose smile warmed her heart, whose touch sent shivers down her spine, and who was definitely not available…

She sighed, stood up, and made her way to bed.

At least all those 'man thoughts' had helped her shut away the feelings of loss that had hit her so hard at the hospital.

And she didn't really need a man. A housekeeper would be far better. The boys could kick footballs at kindy and school, and, anyway, she'd been quite good at soccer at school herself.

She'd kick footballs with them!

And just to prove she could, next morning saw her at the park down at the bottom of the hill, where children of all ages congregated to play—football kicking being only one of the activities.

She'd pushed the boys down in their stroller, although they'd both protested they were big enough to walk. Which they were, but she'd doubted they'd be happy walking back up the hill when they were tired from their play.

A cone-shaped, spider-web climbing frame soon became a favourite, and they were carefully negotiating their separate ways across the ropes when Marty turned up, sent on from the house by Ned.

'I just called in to give you an update on Izzy and George,' he said, smiling and waving at the two boys as he spoke.

'George?' echoed Emma.

Marty turned to grin at her.

'Exactly what I said, but I'm assured old-fashioned names are coming back,' Marty told her. 'I suppose we should be glad it wasn't Alfred.'

Emma laughed, although when she thought about it…

'Actually, I don't mind Alfie.'

'You *can't* be serious!' Marty said, then he dived forward to scoop up Xavier as he fell towards the soft sand beneath the climbing frame.

Emma watched as he set a far from worried little boy

back on the ropes, then stood back as another adult rushed towards his child.

An older child, a boy of about seven, was trying to push his sister off her perch above him, and as Emma watched the girl fell and the man hauled what was presumably his son off the ropes and smacked him, yelling at him for his actions at the same time.

Marty stepped forward, fists clenched, but Emma caught his arm.

He shook her off, but her touch must have calmed him down for he walked away, but not before Emma had seen his face, ashen with shock.

Or memories?

She gathered up her boys, who'd stopped climbing to look at the sobbing child, and followed Marty to where he'd dropped down onto a bench under a shady tree.

Should she say something?

Ask why it had upset him so badly?

Or did she need to ask?

He'd been a foster child, presumably taken from his family.

Because of an abusive father?

'I should have stepped in,' he said.

'And done what? Punched the man in front of his children? Met violence with violence in front of a dozen children?'

She sat beside him and rested her hand on his knee.

'I think he smacked the boy more out of shock than anger. He saw the girl fall and reacted. He was comforting both children when we left.'

Marty nodded, then moved his shoulders as if to shift a burden.

'I know no one likes to see a child being smacked, but why did you react to it like that?' she asked, though she doubted she'd get an answer. For all his outgoing, friendly manner, he was a very private man.

He didn't answer for so long she thought he wouldn't, but then he said, very quietly, 'There was violence in my home—my birth home. My father had an uncontrollable temper and flew into rages at the slightest provocation.'

He'd been looking into the distance but now he turned to her.

'It's in me, too, Emma, that rage. It's in me too.'

'Nonsense,' she said calmly, but he was already on his feet.

'Who's for ice cream?' he called to the two little boys, who were back on the climbing frame.

He got the response he wanted when they ran towards him, and he took a hand of each to lead them to the ice-cream van that was parked, almost permanently, on the other side of the park.

'I'll bring them back safely,' he said to Emma.

She smiled at him and said, 'I didn't doubt it for a minute—there's no one I'd rather trust my boys to than you, Marty Graham.'

But as she watched them walk away, she sighed.

Was friendship always so complicated?

Or was this friendship more complicated than usual because, deep down, she'd have liked it to be more than that?

Of course, it was, but her feelings towards Marty were so tangled up with who they both were—she remembering the pain of a lost love and he, now she understood, fearing his own genetic heritage.

Could love flourish when they both had the darkness of the past to contend with?

Could she take the risk…?

CHAPTER SEVEN

GOING TO WORK seemed something of an anticlimax after the excitements of the weekend, but once there Emma found it soothing to be back in a familiar environment, and even welcomed the rush of the busy morning—patients who hadn't wanted to waste their own precious time over the weekend in the local A and E came rolling in with a variety of complaints.

'Half these people should be visiting their GP,' Helen, no doubt suffering broken sleep patterns given her advanced pregnancy, grumbled.

'Or have come in earlier,' Emma said, having just admitted a small girl with a severe headache and the suggestion of a rash appearing on her body.

'Has she had her meningococcal vaccination?' Emma had asked the concerned parents.

'Oh, no, we don't believe in that kind of thing,' the mother had replied, while Emma had cursed under her breath and hoped it was just an infection that could be cleared up with antibiotics.

But she'd ordered a lumbar puncture to collect a sample of cerebrospinal fluid and in the meantime put the child on a strong antibiotic drip. And she'd spoken to the mother about the importance of vaccinations, not only to protect the individual child but to stop many childhood diseases reaching epidemic proportions once again.

She knew the woman hadn't listened—knew also it wasn't because she was concerned for her child. No, this particular parent had made a stand and had no intention of changing her mind on the subject.

Recognising a lost cause, and admitting to herself that everyone was entitled to their opinion, Emma had walked away, though inwardly seething. Aware she couldn't meet another patient in that state, she'd headed for the tea-room to calm down.

Only to find Marty ensconced in the most comfortable armchair. In fact, the *only* comfortable armchair, the room seemingly furnished with odds and ends of rejected chairs no one else wanted.

She glared at him and he held up his hands.

'Hey, what have *I* done?'

Sat in the chair I wanted.

No, she couldn't use such an inane excuse for her temper.

She made herself a coffee—instant.

'One day I'll buy a decent coffee machine for this place,' she muttered to herself.

'Someone would probably pinch it,' Marty said laconically from the depths of the armchair. 'Is it instant coffee that's got you all steamed up or something else?'

'Of course it's not instant coffee, although I hate the stuff,' she stormed. 'It's parents who don't believe in vaccinating their children. Honestly, Marty, they must never read a paper, never listen to the news to not know how much danger they put not only their own child in but other children in too. I know they have good reasons or beliefs, but if they'd ever seen a child with meningococcal—a child who's lost a limb, or his hearing, or even died, surely they would agree it's better to be safe than sorry.'

He smiled the lazy smile that did funny things to her heart.

'As you said, they have their reasons or beliefs, and they've freedom of choice because we're not a police state—yet.'

Resisting an urge to throw her coffee at him, she settled into the next best chair, comfortable enough if you knew to sit on the left side so the loose spring on the right didn't get you.

'Maybe we should be in some instances,' she muttered darkly, although she knew she didn't mean it. 'Anyway, what are you doing here?'

'Brought you a family update,' he said, not smiling now but she knew from his eyes he was still amused by her tantrum. 'Mother and baby are both doing very well. The local GPs in Wetherby have offered to cover the hospital for Mac so he can stay down in Retford for as long as he feels he's needed. Hallie and Nikki will stay on for the week. I'll work out when I'll be off duty, so I can fly down and take them home.'

'So all's well that ends well,' Emma said with a smile. 'That's terrific. Will they transfer the baby here when he's old enough for us to cope with him in our PICU?'

Marty shook his head.

'I don't know for certain, but as he'd still be an hour away from their home if he's here, I can't see the point. They might as well stay there until he's due for discharge.'

It was a nice, normal conversation, so why did Emma feel it held undercurrents she couldn't understand?

She drank her much-maligned coffee, improving it slightly by dipping gingernut biscuits into it, so aware of Marty across from her, her nerve endings were screaming.

He'd lapsed into silence, which made things worse. Marty was usually good at casual banter—far better than she was. Having worn out the coffee conversation, *and* parents who didn't vaccinate their children, she had no idea where to start a new one.

Marty had sat forward—perhaps he was going to help out with some idle chatter.

Gossip, local news.

No such luck, for he fixed those blue eyes, serious now, on her face, and asked, 'Did you lose a baby? Before you had the twins?'

She couldn't speak, just stared at him. How on earth could he have picked that up?

And what business was it of his?

But she knew that was unfair—he hadn't asked out of curiosity but because he cared, because he was a caring man.

And suddenly it was easy…

'Not long after Simon died,' she told him quietly, glad she'd used up all her tears for the baby the night they'd brought Izzy in. 'I was stressed, lost in grief, I suppose, and didn't recognise the symptoms. I was only twenty-one weeks, the baby didn't have much chance of surviving and it didn't. She didn't.'

Well, he *had* asked, Marty muttered in his mind. And if staying in the chair—not crossing the room to take her in his arms and hold her—was the hardest thing he'd ever done, then too bad.

'You saw me crying—the night Izzy was brought in?' Emma had paled at his question but her voice was steady.

He had to nod—agree—because he *had* seen the hastily wiped-away tears and his heart had been gripped by pain.

But Emma seemed less upset now, so maybe he hadn't made a mistake in talking to her about it.

She was looking directly at him, and spoke slowly, as if finding the right words was difficult.

'I think I hadn't properly grieved for the baby,' she admitted. 'I was still so lost, still hurting over Simon, so the other night, when it all came rushing back, well…'

She half smiled, and he marvelled at her bravery.

'When something like that happens, at first you're angry—the "why me" thing. I'd been exactly the same with Simon, though more "why him". Then losing the baby, his baby, I felt as if my world had ended a second time and I just shut down.'

She paused, and though he ached to hold her, to comfort her—protect her really—he stayed still and silent, aware she hadn't finished and probably needed to say more.

'In a way it was a good thing, the tears the other night. They released something that had been pent up inside me for too long,' she finished, standing up and crossing to the sink to wash out her cup, returning the biscuits to their tin.

Her movement told him the subject was closed—probably forever. But how could he not love this small woman who had been through so much, yet soldiered on, wanting only the best for her patients and the very best for her boys, her father, her family?

A woman who trusted him with her children…

'I've got to get back to work,' she said, telling him in no uncertain terms that the intimacies were over.

Although…

She'd stopped at the door and turned back towards him.

'And now I've told you my last bit of secret pain, sometime you can tell me yours.'

He was dumbfounded.

'Secret pain?' he echoed, and she smiled and nodded.

'That innocent act doesn't fool me for one minute, Marty Graham. Next time it's your turn to talk.'

Emma returned to work in a more positive state of mind. She'd vented her anger and shared something very personal with a friend—something she hadn't done for a very long time.

A friend?

The tiny whisper in her head was nothing more than wishful thinking. Marty was a friend, full stop.

Fortunately, before that devious voice could whisper again, she was diverted by two patients, herded into A and E by a large and obviously angry man.

'Bloody idiots,' he said, waving his hand towards the two teenagers who'd sunk down onto the nearest chairs, blood visible on the hands that held their respective heads.

'Fighting in the school grounds—which is banned,' the man continued, 'and over which football team is the best, of all things. What does *that* say about sport?'

Helen was there, leading one of the combatants towards a cubicle, while Joss appeared to take the other one.

'I think it's only minor damage—a lot of blood from head wounds, but we need to get them checked out,' the man said, then, as if remembering his manners, he held out his hand.

'I'm Andy Richards, assistant sports master at the high school. You're new here, aren't you?'

Emma took his hand—a nice firm hand.

'I'm Emma Crawford, and, yes, I'm new in town.'

He studied her for a minute.

'You're not by any chance Ned Crawford's daughter?'

Emma nodded.

'Do you know my father?'

Andy grinned at her.

'No, not had the pleasure, but if I've heard one story about what Ned and my father got up to in the "old days"—' he gave the words inverted commas with his fingers '—I've heard a dozen. Dad hasn't been well lately, which might explain why he hasn't realised Ned's daughter is in town. I know he'd love to meet you.'

'Then maybe he'd also like to see my father,' Emma suggested. 'He's back in town with me. I'm a single mum so he looks after my boys when I'm at work, and generally takes care of things. But I know he wants to catch up with old friends. I'd better see to your two lads now, but if you give me your father's number, Dad can give him a call.'

Andy produced a pen and a rather grubby piece of paper from his pocket and jotted down a number.

'I live there too—with Dad,' he said, and she had a feeling he was telling that bit to her, not as a message to her father.

She put the note in her pocket and hurried to the first cubicle, where Angie had cleaned up a forehead wound and was busy putting plastic strips across it.

'I don't think it needs stitching,' she said. 'What do you think?'

Emma agreed with her and left her to finish the dressing. But the second combatant had come off the worse for wear, a cut close to his eye definitely needing stitching, and he had enough bruising on his face, especially near the temple, for Emma to decide a CAT scan was necessary.

'It's purely precautionary,' she told their patient. 'I'll put a temporary dressing on that cut until after I've seen the scan.'

Not that the scan would make any difference to her treatment of the wound, but she felt it was more urgent than a few stitches.

She left Joss with him to arrange the scan, then crossed the room to explain to Andy what they were doing.

'It won't take long, but if you need to get back, we could phone when he's ready to leave.'

Andy shook his head.

'I'll stay—duty of care and all that.'

She smiled at him.

'Something we're all only too aware of these days,' she agreed.

It was close to an hour before she'd finally stitched the cut, and between patients had stopped a few times to speak to Andy. He seemed a really nice guy, and if he lived with his father, maybe he *was* single—

What on earth was she thinking?

Was she really stalking the single men of Braxton?

Hadn't she decided she could kick a football with the best of men?

And that she'd get a housekeeper to free up her father? After all, she could afford one…

Or was she using the 'single men' idea in her head to stop her thinking of Marty?

Some questions had no answers.

The days flowed smoothly after that, and Emma realised she was getting into the routine of the hospital, fitting in as she learnt the ways that things were done, and feeling comfortable at work. She'd found she liked being part of a smaller hospital where the different departments all mixed far more than they did in city hospitals.

And it was easier to follow the progress of a patient she'd admitted than it had been in the labyrinth of wards where she'd worked before.

Yes, all in all, it was great.

Until late on Friday afternoon, when one of the coastguard officers called the emergency line.

'We've got a seaman badly injured on a large container ship east of Wetherby. I've alerted helicopter rescue but we'll need to drop a doctor on board to check him out before he can be moved.'

Emma sighed.

If there was one thing she hated more than winch practice it was being winched onto the deck of a moving ship. Not that she'd done it for real, but the practice sessions on Sydney Harbour had been terrifying.

But it was her call. The doctor who'd come in on the

swing shift was too old for helicopter work but would cover her in A and E.

She took the phone.

'How badly hurt? And do we know how it happened?'

'They've come through some bad weather and it's still a bit rough out there, but he was checking the chains on the containers when one moved and trapped him somehow. We're thinking crush injuries to his legs and chest, and probable internal injuries.'

She *had* to go!

She thanked the man absentmindedly, her mind racing as she thought of drugs and equipment she might need. She could already hear the helicopter approaching but by the time it put down she was ready for it, scrambling on board with Mark's helping hand.

Mark handed her a flight suit and helmet, and she hurriedly pulled them on, replacing the sneakers she wore to work with the sturdy boots, her pair now marked with an E for Emma.

And lastly the helmet.

But she no sooner had it strapped into place than Marty's voice came blasting through it.

'Are you up to this?' he demanded. 'Have you had marine rescue training? Mark's a qualified paramedic, he can go down to the boat if you're not sure.'

Put out by his doubts about her ability, her replies were naturally tetchy.

'Yes, I am up to it,' she snapped, 'and, yes, wonder of wonders, I've done marine rescue training, and if you think landing on a small motor boat on Sydney Harbour in gale-force winds is easier than landing on the massive deck of a container ship, then you've never tried it.'

She paused before remembering the last bit of his conversation.

'And although Mark's a great paramedic, just maybe

someone who's had a container land on him actually needs a doctor.'

A silent clapping from Mark made heat rise to her cheeks. She'd broadcast her conversation to all of them, rather than holding the button that would have taken it only to Marty.

'Stop it,' she hissed at Mark, who was grinning with delight.

'No way,' he whispered, his mic well away from his lips. 'The boss needs to be put in his place now and then. He's far too protective of all of us.'

Which, Emma decided as she tightened the straps on the harness that would hook her to the winch, was probably a good thing.

And another good thing was that it wasn't personal. Marty behaved protectively towards all his crew, not just her.

They saw the slowly moving vessel within minutes of crossing the coastline, and Emma watched as it grew bigger and bigger. Then it was beneath them, Marty matching his speed to it, holding the chopper at a steady pace above a mark the crew had painted on the deck. Mark clipped her and her bag to the winch before opening the side door, and after a quick prayer to any god that might have been hovering nearby, she sat in the doorway, took a deep breath, signalled she was ready to go and began her careful descent.

The wind wasn't as strong as she'd expected, but it gusted unpredictably, teasing her with a push or shove every now and then.

The crewmen awaiting her were close now, their excitement rising in their voices. Someone caught her legs and guided them down onto the deck, where Emma unclipped herself and her bag and sent the wire back up for the stretcher.

None of them had had any doubt that it would be needed.

Her patient lay in the shadow of the towers of containers, and Emma could see the one that had moved slightly out of alignment, apparently pushing him against the next, though what he'd been doing between the two she couldn't fathom.

Not her problem.

One of the crewmen, wearing a uniform that suggested rank, explained what had happened in careful English, then added, 'He was conscious at first, but then not. I do not think his head was injured, but he is not speaking.'

Even before examining the extent of his injuries, Emma could believe he'd passed out because of pain. Which was better as far as she was concerned. Giving pain relief to a patient likely to be heading straight into Theatre was always tricky.

She knelt to examine the man, lifting temporary dressings off his legs, shuddering at the damage that had been done.

Airway!

His breathing was rapid but shallow and his lips slightly blue. It hardly needed the misalignment of the trachea to tell her the cause.

Tension pneumothorax.

She found the needle she needed and inserted it into the second rib space on the damaged side, drew up some air into the syringe, then carefully withdrew the needle, leaving the cannula in place.

Air rushing out told her she'd done the right thing, although she knew this was only temporary relief for the blood vessels in the man's chest. She secured the tube, fixed a loose dressing over it, and checked his blood pressure.

Far too low, but the best thing she could do was get

him on the stretcher and into the chopper, where she could work on him as they flew him to hospital.

With the help of the crew, they slid the two sides of the stretcher under him and clicked the parts together, then wrapped him in the protective wings and fastened the straps that held him securely in place.

Worried that a vertical lift might injure him further, she radioed up to let Dave know she was sending him up, attaching four straps to the winch wire, and signalling to lift.

As ever, it seemed to take an age for the winch wire to descend again for her, but when it did, a crewman handed it to her and she slid the little seat between her legs and clipped on, signalling again to lift.

By the time she unclipped back in the helicopter, Mark had the stretcher secure and a cannula inserted in the man's hand, ready for fluid resuscitation, and an oxygen mask on his face.

'Braxton or straight to Retford?' Marty asked.

'Retford,' Emma told him, aware that the Braxton Hospital didn't have the surgical teams the man would need.

Working carefully, she and Mark removed the man's boots, cutting the laces to ease them off his feet before cutting away his socks and the tattered clothing on his legs. They irrigated the wounds, squirting most of the loose debris away, but had to resort to tweezers for the deeper pieces.

'It's a mercy he's unconscious,' Mark said as they wrapped clean dressings around the injured limbs. The tibia was broken on both legs and from the position of the break, Emma suspected the fibula would also have suffered. But the breaks were above the ankles, which would make surgery and recovery simpler.

His thighs were less damaged.

'Probably because his right hip bone and pelvis bore the brunt of the pressure,' Mark said, but for all the IV fluids they were pumping into him, his blood pressure remained worryingly low.

Had a major blood vessel been impacted when his chest had been caught by the great weight? But wouldn't he have already bled out if that was the case? The question tormented Emma.

Should they put down in Braxton first so a surgeon could open him up to look for a rupture?

'ETA Retford thirty minutes.'

Marty's message decided her. Retford was definitely the best option.

She radioed her findings to Retford Hospital, adding her suspicion about internal bleeding, so was pleased to see a crash team waiting as they touched down.

The man was rushed straight into Theatre, and she sat in the doorway of the helicopter to complete her paperwork. One copy had accompanied the man, but this second sheet was required for the Search and rescue service records.

'You want to come and see George?' Marty asked, dropping down to sit beside her.

Did she?

Her boys had been premmie, but only by six weeks, but she'd still spent enough time in a PICU to know she didn't really like the places. There was always a positive vibe, and few premmie babies were ever lost, but the sight of the wee mites in their cribs brought back memories of the baby she had lost—the baby who had been too small to save.

'No, thanks,' she said, but probably so long after he'd asked the question that he'd guess what she'd been thinking.

'No worries, but I'm popping in to see the family, so why don't you go over to the canteen? Dave and Mark will be there. We'll leave in thirty minutes unless there's another callout, in which case I'll contact you.'

He jumped to the ground and walked away, leaving Emma feeling very alone, and more than slightly put out.

Normally, Marty would touch her shoulder as he passed her, or at least turn around and wave if he was walking away.

Had she let him down, not going to see George?

Oh, for heaven's sake, get your head on straight, she berated herself. There was no reason on earth why Marty should wave or touch her shoulder. In fact, it was far better that he didn't because if either thing had happened it would have affected her body in ways she didn't want—her shoulder would have felt warm where his hand had been, while a wave, or the smile that always accompanied it, would have sent shivers down her spine.

But physical reactions stemmed from attraction—that's all it was. After all, he was an attractive man—hadn't half the women in town been attracted to him at some time?

And if it was attraction, then all she had to do was resist it…

Marty headed straight for the PICU, knowing at least one of the family would be there.

Mac and Nikki were.

'Hallie's taken Izzy to get some clothes—little essentials like underwear and nightdresses and stuff to wear during the day,' Mac explained.

'And I'm in charge of George,' Nikki announced. 'Of talking to him, I mean. You have to talk to the babies, did you know that? I've been telling him about Wetherby and how we'll play in the sand when he gets a bit bigger and how I'll help him make sandcastles with moats around them and even volcanoes.'

'Might be a while before you get to volcanoes,' Mac put in drily.

Marty laughed, then bent to examine his new nephew.

'He certainly looks good, given how premmie he is,' he said, and Mac nodded.

'He's the unit champ already,' he said, and the note of pride in Mac's voice pierced through a special shield Marty had wrapped around his heart.

No babies! he reminded himself, but he knew the wound remained and always would.

But Nikki was pointing out his tiny toes, and Marty found a smile for this girl he'd known since she'd been born.

'You were in a crib like this, and you had even tinier toes,' he told her, and she laughed.

Which was a good way to leave them, Marty decided.

'Well, I'd better get the crew back to Braxton,' he said, kissing Nikki and patting Mac on the shoulder. 'Give Izzy my love, and Nikki, tell Hallie to phone me when you're both ready to go home.'

'I can phone you. I do have a phone, you know,' Nikki told him, so he was smiling as he left.

Still smiling when he reached the chopper to find Emma sitting where he'd left her.

'Didn't you want refreshment?' he asked, and she looked up as if he'd startled her.

Her eyes met his and messages he couldn't understand seemed to flash between them, messages that made him feel hot, and light-headed at the same time.

Made him want to close the distance between them in long strides and take her in his arms…

Kiss the eyes that sent him messages…

Was he nuts?

This was Emma.

Emma, who'd already suffered two terrible losses in her

life. No way could he cause her more disruption. Yes, he was attracted to her—maybe very attracted to her—but…

But what?

Love?

He shook his head in an attempt to clear it, aware that this wasn't the first time that word had filled it when he thought of Emma…

She watched him walk towards her, feeling such a mix of emotions she didn't have a clue which one dominated.

Attraction was in there for sure, but it was more than that. It was something deep inside her gut, some instinct that was telling her stupid things, telling her this man was important in her life and—worse—that she wanted him there.

He *is* in your life, stupid, she told herself. He's a friend, a colleague, almost a relation if Ned's friendship with Carrie leads to something more…

He'd reached her now, and settled himself beside her in the doorway.

'Tell me?'

It was gently asked, his voice deep and slightly husky, and it would have been foolishly naïve to ask him what he meant.

'I met Simon, my husband, when I started work as an intern in the ED of a big Sydney hospital. He was senior staff and I knew he'd barely notice me, but he did. I'd already noticed him—thought him wonderful, and although at the time that was more hero worship of a junior to a very accomplished man, I found out he *was* wonderful. He was everything a top ED specialist should be—kind, caring, compassionate yet firm with drunks and time-wasters.'

She glanced at Marty, wondering how he was taking this—really wondering why he'd asked…

'Tough competition for any bloke coming along now,' he said, and she felt a little spurt of anger.

'Well, it shouldn't worry you, because you're not, are you?'

'Not what?' he asked, all innocence.

'Competition! You don't do commitment, remember?' she snapped. 'Now, do you want me to finish or not?'

Talking about Simon had stirred up the memories she usually kept tucked carefully away in a box in the back of her mind, but now she saw him in her mind's eye, striding through the ED, flashing a smile here, touching a shoulder there, always so equable, so patient—always with time for everyone.

Especially for her.

Always for her…

'Please,' Marty said, and it took her a moment to remember what she'd asked.

Could she go on?

Best if she did.

Hadn't Dad been telling her she should talk about the man she'd loved, if only for the boys' sake?

'We got married; I kept working until I fell pregnant then Simon began to get headaches, not telling me at first—not, in fact, until he'd seen a specialist, had all the scans and tests, and been told he only had six weeks to live.'

Try as she might, she couldn't shut the box of memories now and her eyes blurred with tears.

'I've told you most of the rest—the "why me" reaction that is purely selfish, then living with a loved one's pain, feeling his suffering and knowing I couldn't ease it, pretending all the time that life goes on when, really, it doesn't—it stands still, seemingly forever…'

'And the boys?'

The question was so out of left field, so startling, she forgot her tears, and just stared at the man who'd asked it.

'You were pregnant but you lost that baby,' he reminded her gently, moving closer to put his arm around her shoulders.

The pain she'd been feeling receded.

'I think the day Simon had the news, he went to see Stephen. They'd been contemporaries at university. Simon and I—we'd talked about our family, what we'd like in the way of kids. We knew we wanted more than one, so just in case I ever decided to have another one, he had some sperm frozen.'

Emma paused, wondering if talking about stuff you didn't want to talk about really was cathartic, because somehow now she was feeling better.

'For a long time after I'd lost the first baby, having another just wasn't on the agenda. I was still grieving for Simon and for his baby—our baby—as well, so I'd completely forgotten the frozen sperm.'

She paused, thinking back to that momentous day when Dad had suggested using it.

And smiled.

'Dad suggested it, promised to help, to mind the baby while I kept on working. It was three years after Simon's death and I must have been ready, because suddenly it was the best idea I'd ever heard. I went to see Stephen and the rest, as they say, is history. The very best part of it was that I conceived not one but two babies.'

Marty drew her closer and clasped her hands in his, aware how hard it would have been for her to tell this story. But she'd been through so much loss and pain *his* heart hurt, thinking about it.

But now he understood her detached approach to the

search for a father for the twins. She'd suffered too much to want to love again—to risk that terrible pain…

So he sat and held her, felt her warmth, knew whatever it was between them could not continue.

Except for friendship.

That he could provide…

CHAPTER EIGHT

BY THE TIME they touched down at the base in Braxton, Emma was well and truly off duty.

'You want a lift home?' Mark asked, as the pair of them stripped off their flight suits and hung them on the pegs in the big shed that was the headquarters of Braxton Search and Rescue.

But Marty was right behind them, and he spoke before Emma could reply.

'Don't worry, I'll take her, it's on my way.'

'Do I get to choose?' Emma muttered, then realised it was a stupid thing to have said. She'd far rather Marty drove her home, although wouldn't it be better if she went with Mark?

No temptation that way, no time to study the way Marty's hands held the steering wheel, the precise but effortless way he drove; no need to sit there revelling in the warmth that just being close to him always provided. No need to torture herself.

Especially after the way she'd poured out her heart to him!

But while these ridiculous thoughts tumbled through her head the matter had been decided. While she'd been thinking of his hands on the steering wheel, and whether or not she regretted telling him about Simon, he'd answered her question with a sharp, inarguable 'No'.

Feeling aggrieved, she followed him out to his vehicle, clambering into the big four-wheel drive.

'Where does Mark live?' she asked, still put out by his making her decision for her.

'Way out the other side of town and he'll have his wife and kids waiting for him. They always hear the chopper go over so they know exactly when he'll be home.'

'Is this your subtle way of telling me he's a married man? Warning me off?'

He didn't answer, so she added, 'Anyway, I already knew that. He's told me all about his family.'

Marty sighed, then pulled over to the side of the road and turned off the engine.

He stared out through the windscreen for a few moments then said, 'I can't keep doing this.'

As he was still studying the road ahead and perhaps the bush that surrounded them, Emma could only see his profile and it wasn't telling her anything.

'This what?' she asked, and he turned towards her, reaching out as if to touch her.

'*This*,' he said. 'This being close to you, finding excuses to be near you, aching for you in every cell in my body but knowing I've no right to even be touching you.'

Emma turned to fully face him and caught his hands in hers.

'Why haven't you?' she asked. 'Just tell me why.'

He shook his head and went back to staring out the windscreen.

Heart pounding, Emma undid the clasp of her seatbelt and manoeuvred across the seat to get as close as she could to him.

She put her hand on his cheek and turned his face towards her, then leaned forward and kissed him on the lips.

They were warm, his lips, but still, and for a long,

dreadful moment she thought she'd done the wrong thing—totally wrecked whatever it was they had.

Or didn't have…

Then his lips responded and he turned his body, reaching out to draw her close, to hold her in an iron clasp while his lips devoured hers, feasting on them—a starving man finding food…

Her heat matched his, burning in her body, lips opening, tongues tangling, little moans coming from one or other of them, maybe both, Emma didn't know.

She only knew that this was what she'd wanted, yet hadn't wanted, what she'd missed, but hadn't wanted to miss.

The engine noise of an approaching car broke them apart, and they both straightened in their seats, *both* looking through the windscreen now, panting slightly.

The car passed and Marty started the engine of his vehicle, pulling carefully back onto the road.

Emma re-buckled her seatbelt, too confused to speak, hardly daring to look at the man who'd aroused such fire in her.

But was it only fire?

Need?

Lust?

Or something more?

Fire and need would be okay. Maybe even lust. They could have an affair, try to keep it quiet. They spent so much time together anyway, maybe it would go unnoticed…

Except by her father, who would be the one minding the boys while she was with Marty, which would mean putting more responsibility on him when she was trying to free him up to live his own life.

'I can't have an affair.'

She blurted out the end result of all her torturous thoughts as Marty pulled up outside her house.

'It wouldn't be fair on Dad. Especially now when he's just begun to have a little bit of social life himself.'

Marty turned towards her, one side of his mouth lifting in a rueful smile.

'I was about to say the same thing,' he said, reaching out to cup her cheek in one hand and rub his thumb across her undoubtedly swollen lips. 'I couldn't do that to you. Couldn't have you join the list as "another one of Marty's women" because you are way, way more than that to me.'

He shook his head, not smiling now.

'So, we're stuck, aren't we?'

Unless it wasn't an affair, the treacherous voice in Emma's head whispered, and it was her turn to shake her head. Getting married again was a sensible, practical idea for her and she had no doubt she'd grow to love the man she married.

In time…

But the thing she didn't want was passion, because that way heartbreak lay…

Yet whatever it was that had flared between her and Marty was definitely passion, the kind, she feared, that would deepen and spread like wildfire through her body, steal the heart she'd have to grow again, and fill her life.

Which meant commitment—the one thing Marty didn't want.

She leaned across and kissed his cheek.

'Thanks for the lift,' she said, and slid out of the car.

Marty drove home, his body throbbing, his mind in turmoil as anger at his foolish action raged back and forth.

He'd stopped the car because the urge to kiss the woman he'd been with—to hold her in his arms and feel her body against his and, yes, to kiss her senseless—had been so strong he'd feared he'd have an accident if he'd kept driving.

Had it been Mark's offer to drive Emma home that had lit the touch-paper?

Or had it happened earlier when he'd walked back to the chopper and seen her sitting in the doorway—watching him. Something he couldn't read in her eyes. Something he couldn't read yet still excited him.

Then she'd told him about her husband—about Simon's death—had poured out her heart to him and he'd…

What?

Whatever, he'd stopped the car to cool down—to get his head together—and the damn woman had kissed him.

Not just kissed him but responded to his kisses with white-hot fire that had burned through his body like a fever.

Which left him where exactly?

Apart from frustrated as hell…

He'd just have to avoid her whenever possible, quite easy, really, a lot of his flights didn't involve a doctor…

He remembered her little boys, their hands placed so trustingly in his when they'd gone for ice cream, and he thought his heart might break.

But his sudden surge of temper just before that happy moment had reminded him genetics ruled.

Okay, so he probably wouldn't have hit the bloke for smacking his kid, even without Emma's touch on his arm, but he'd wanted to…

Yet hadn't Emma said, even after seeing that, that she'd trust him more than anyone with her boys?

Could he get past the so hated, yet still so vivid image of his father's raised arm, his mother falling with the baby…

Could he deny his genes?

* * *

Refusing to think about what had happened in the car and adamant not to dwell on her reaction to Marty's kiss, Emma had marched into the house determined on action.

'You're home early,' her father called to her. 'The boys are still asleep.'

'That's great,' she said, joining him in the kitchen where the sight of him, ironing board out, carefully ironing small T-shirts strengthened her resolve.

'What afternoons does the bridge club meet?' she asked.

'And why would you want to know?' he asked, not looking at her as he folded the now ironed shirt into a neat square.

He was *so* much better at this housework stuff than she was!

'Because I'm about to employ a housekeeper,' she announced. 'I've been thinking it over for a while, and now we've settled in up here, it's time I made a move. Not full time, I wouldn't think, but a few days a week, and, no, it's not for your sake but for mine.'

'I'm not good enough?' her father teased.

'You're too damned good,' Emma retorted. 'So much so I've taken you for granted for far too long. I know I would never have coped alone when Simon died, let alone even thought of having children, but I'm fine now, and you need your life back.'

'But—'

Emma held up her hand.

'No, don't tell me how much you've loved doing it or any other nonsense. I know you love the kids and me, but we can't be your whole life, not anymore. You deserve better than that, Dad, and it's your turn now.'

Her father picked up another tiny shirt, smoothed it flat on the ironing board, and carefully pushed the iron across it, and only when it was done and folded, sitting on top of the small pile, did he look at her again.

'I *have* enjoyed it,' he said, smiling at her. 'Every last minute of it, although we've had some hairy times, haven't we?'

Emma smiled at him, thinking of the night Xavier had had croup, and her father had been on a rare night out and she'd driven to the house where he'd been having dinner with friends to leave Hamish with him before taking Xavier to the hospital.

'Some,' she admitted.

She made herself a sandwich and a cup of tea then retired to the room they'd allocated as an office in the big, rambling, old house. Setting the snack down on the desk, she pulled out the book where they kept phone numbers, knowing Carrie's number would be in it.

But Carrie was in Retford, and possibly in the PICU where no phones were allowed…

Would Joss be home? She'd be off duty by now, and as she'd grown up in Braxton she'd be sure to know someone who'd know someone who might be able to help.

Joss put her on to her mother, Mrs Carstairs, who was only too happy to recommend a couple of women, giving Emma the names and numbers, and adding, 'Christine, the first one, probably needs the money most,' she said, 'and she's wonderful with children. She used to work at the childcare centre until the new regulations came in about all helpers needing at least six months at a training course before they could work there. All nonsense, of course, because six months at a college doesn't help you comfort a child who's not feeling well, or tell you when a child needs a cuddle.'

Emma smiled at the woman's disgust but she understood what she was saying, although she was pretty sure these days the college courses for early childhood education would include a fair amount of work in kindergartens, spending hands-on time with children.

As predicted, Christine was delighted at the idea and, yes, she could call around at Emma's house in an hour, by which time the boys would certainly be awake, and hopefully in good moods after their sleeps.

Research time…

Emma opened her laptop and searched for childcare wages. She'd known for some time she'd have to get a local accountant but had been putting it off. If she was going to become an employer, she'd need him to work out things like superannuation. But at least that could wait until Carrie got back, or she could ask the nurses at work. Right now, she had to pin her father down to what day the bridge club met, and whether he wanted to take up bowls again.

And if, at the back of her mind, there was a whispered suggestion that employing a housekeeper could also free her up to have more of a life outside work and childcare, she ignored it.

Although that Andy Richards had seemed a nice guy…

And wouldn't finding someone else, even on a temporary basis, help her ignore her futile feelings for Marty?

Probably not, but at least she could try…

Marty flew back to Retford a few days later in his own chopper to collect Hallie and Nikki, delivering them safely to Wetherby and deciding to stay the night.

Sometimes a bit of time with Pop in the shed, a night in his old bedroom, and a chat about nothing in particular with Hallie got his head straightened out. But it was not to be. Although he felt relaxed and happy in his old home, he also realised the problem that was Emma would never straighten out.

The best strategy, as he'd decided after the fateful kiss, was avoidance and although he dismissed moving to another base—he's miss his family too much—if he kept busy, and found another woman to squire around town, then surely he wouldn't see too much of her and that would be that.

But fate conspired against him.

He thought Carrie's birthday celebration, on a Saturday night, would be okay because the girls were throwing the party for her. Marty knew Carrie was seeing a bit of Ned so he would be there for sure, and without the girls to babysit, Emma would be stuck at home.

Of course, that was before he'd heard about Christine, or learned that she was always happy to do extra hours, babysitting.

Neither had he heard about Andy.

Well, he knew Andy, had been at school with him, and although they didn't see much of each other these days, they were still quite friendly.

Until his old school-mate arrived at the party with Emma, so it was a double shock. Seeing Emma, and, what was worse, seeing her with another man—particularly a man he liked and respected…

He prayed for a callout, because there was no other way he'd get out of his sister's birthday party. But no matter how many times he checked that his phone was turned on and, no, there'd been no missed messages, no call came.

So he made himself useful, filling people's glasses, passing around the canapes the girls had prepared, chatting to Pop and Hallie, and Carrie's friends from school. Avoiding Emma and Andy and the group of locals who would normally have been his chosen company at any party.

But there were only so many glasses to be filled, and

the canapés ran out so he sought refuge on the back veranda, only to back away through the door when he saw one of his nieces out there in the passionate embrace of what was probably a spotty youth.

He could leave.

He'd done his duty.

He found Mandy—so it was Molly on the veranda—in the kitchen and was about to say goodbye when his phone buzzed in his pocket.

He dug it out and positively beamed at it.

'Have to go, pet,' he said. 'Lovely party, say goodbye to your mum for me.'

He kissed her cheek and slipped away, hurrying out the back way, so it wasn't until he reached the gate that he realised someone was coming down the steps behind him.

'Can you give me a lift?'

Of course, it was Emma!

'Isn't anyone else ever on callout duty at that hospital?' he demanded, as heat and despair battled in his body.

'Nope,' she said, far too cheerfully. 'You're going to be stuck with me for a couple more months, at least while Paul's still having chemo.'

The reminder made him feel terrible. Paul Robbins, father of four, had been diagnosed with lymphoma and although it was one of the less aggressive forms of the disease, he still had to undergo some treatment.

'What have you heard?' he asked, as he opened the vehicle door for her.

She turned to look at him as the interior lights came on, her face a little pale.

'Possible heart attack, maybe stroke. It was a very confused call, out on some road I've never heard of where there's no ambulance access. An old man in pain—a hermit of some kind? Somewhere between here and Wetherby, is it?'

He nodded, shutting the door as she settled in and hurrying around to the driver's side.

'Ken Irvine, he's an old timber cutter who lives out in the bush.'

Emma had squashed herself as close to the door as possible in case the urge to touch Marty—just to feel the warmth of him—was made harder by an accidental brush of clothing. She'd been watching him—surreptitiously, she hoped—all evening, whilst keeping up with the conversation between Andy and the people he knew.

After all, *she'd* invited Andy, bumping into him down town where she'd been shopping for some new jeans. Thinking, hoping, *needing* a distraction from the man she couldn't have…

Yet the minute Marty had walked in, she'd known it wasn't going to work—that no matter who she saw, or met, they wouldn't ever banish the memories of that kiss.

Which was ridiculous, because that's all it had been—a kiss!

'Do you know the place?' she asked as the silence stretching between them reached snapping point.

'From when I was a kid,' he said. 'I remember going out there the first time with Pop. You could only drive to within about six miles of his hut, then walked in the rest of the way. He had a horse and cart, would you believe, and would drive you back to the car in that. He'd once felled huge cedars in the forest, but now he pulls out old fallen timber and cuts it for firewood. Nowadays, the track gets you to within about two miles of the hut, but he still has the horse and cart to haul the cut wood to your car.'

'How does he exist?' Emma asked. 'What does he do for food? Does he take the horse and cart to town?'

'Until recently he did, although I've a feeling he's stopped coming—maybe his horse died. One of the home care people goes out from time to time to check on him, and he's had a phone connected so he can order anything he needs and someone in town will always take it out. I've sometimes taken my little chopper in there—actually took it in with a couple of friends a year or two ago to clear a space big enough for the rescue helicopter—but on the whole, he'd far rather people stayed away.'

They'd pulled up at the base, where Dave was waiting for them.

'As far as I can make out, they don't know what happened but he'll probably need to be brought back to town for checking,' Dave said. 'He should be kept in town now. He's far too old to be out there on his own.'

Dave looked from Marty to Emma.

'If you've got Emma, do you need me?' he asked. 'It's only that I've left my eldest looking after the younger kids and the baby's not that well.'

Emma looked at Marty—he was the boss in these situations.

'It's fine with me,' she said, and he shrugged.

'Me, too,' he said, but Emma guessed it wasn't all that fine.

Was he wanting to spend as little time with her as she was with him?

Dave had brought her bag from the hospital so she climbed in, settling in Mark's seat, and wondering if Marty would suggest she move up front.

He didn't, which really didn't bother her, although as they flew through the night she realised she wouldn't have minded seeing the forest at night, looking for animals the searchlight might pick out.

It was a short flight, and they landed not far from a small shack, where a light flickered uncertainly.

An old kerosene lantern, Emma realised when she followed Marty into the shack.

Ken had managed to crawl to where the phone stood on a small table, but once there had obviously collapsed. She knelt beside the old man's body while Marty held the lamp a little closer for her.

'This light won't do,' he said, setting the lamp down on the table where the phone must have been. 'I'll see what I can find.'

But Emma knew it wasn't necessary to have more light. Ken was barely conscious, his pulse thready and his breathing raspy and shallow.

Yet he had the strength to grasp her wrist.

'Don' take me from me home,' he whispered. 'Le' me die in me own bed.'

'Marty,' she called softly. 'Can you help me lift him onto his bed?'

He appeared beside her.

'Surely we should be lifting him onto a stretcher?' he asked, and she shook her head.

'He called for help,' Marty persisted.

'I'll take his legs,' Emma said, ignoring his protest.

She leant down towards Ken.

'We'll lift you onto the bed, it shouldn't hurt.'

For a moment, she thought Marty would argue, but in the end he knelt and gently lifted the man into his arms, dispensing with Emma's services and carrying him to the old bed in a corner of the room, wrapping a faded quilt around him to keep him warm.

Emma followed, bending to examine him, seeing the distortion of his face that told of a stroke, the blue colour of his lips, and the old man's struggle to breathe.

She took Ken's hand in both of hers, and held it tightly.

'This is a beautiful, peaceful place,' she said quietly.

Ken smiled.

'Built it all meself,' he told her, and she could still hear pride in the weak, quavery voice.

'Found the clearing when I was cutting big stuff, saw the creek nearby, and knew it was for me.'

The words took a long time to come out, and were indistinct at best, yet Emma knew the old man wanted her—or them—to understand.

'Been a good home,' he said. 'Good life.'

His eyes closed and it seemed as if he dozed, then the hand Emma still held squeezed her fingers.

'You won't leave me?'

Emma gently returned the pressure.

'No way, Ken. Marty and I will be right here.'

The rheumy eyes opened and he looked at her and smiled, a tremulous spread of blueish lips over tobacco-stained teeth.

'Never thought I'd 'ave a pretty girl with me when I died,' he joked, and Emma had to fight to hold back tears.

Had Marty sensed her distress that he joined the conversation?

'Every bloke deserves a pretty girl to be with him at the end,' he told Ken. 'Really, it's the only way to go.'

But although Ken smiled, Emma had heard the tremor in Marty's voice, and knew he, too, was affected.

Marty had found a stool and he'd pulled it over so he sat close to Emma by the bed, and he talked softly, reminding Ken about his visits here. And now and then Ken added memories of his own, about the bush around his hut, the animals who'd shared his life here, deep in the forest.

'You were lucky the bushfire missed you,' Emma said at one stage, and the old man, whose breathing had become raspy and uneven, shook his head.

'Gullies east of range don't burn,' he managed between faltering breaths. 'Worked it out.'

And he smiled…

He was breathing still, deep breaths followed by a pause…

'Cheyne-Stokes,' Marty whispered, and Emma nodded.

In the past it had been known as the death rattle but, whatever its name, they both knew it meant the end was in sight.

The crackle of Marty's radio broke the silence, and as he stood to go outside to answer the call, Emma said, 'I can't leave him.'

'As if we would,' Marty retorted softly, before disappearing into the darkness.

He was back within minutes, sitting down again beside Emma.

'If there's a call I'll have to go,' he said quietly, and she nodded.

'I suppose me too if I'm needed.'

Marty didn't answer, but he slid his arm around her waist and they sat together, keeping vigil over the old man, both praying they could stay so he had company on his last night on earth.

'So talk to me,' Emma murmured to Marty when the old man had drifted into a deep coma. 'Tell me why no commitment? You're a warm, loving person, you're good with kids, why the rule?'

He was silent for so long she began to think he wouldn't answer, then he took his arm from around her waist and held her free hand instead, moving his stool just a little away from her and Ken.

'My father killed my mother, Em,' he said, barely breathing the words so she had to strain to listen, certain Ken wouldn't hear them.

'He killed her and the baby she held in her arms. He lifted up his arm and struck her. I watched her fall and heard the silence—a silence so loud I've never forgotten it. I don't remember if he knelt to touch her, to see if she was dead, although looking back I knew she'd hit the corner of the table in her fall. My father ran howling from the room—gone—and no one knew until I don't know how long later when I was in hospital and someone told me he was dead.'

She used the hand he held to draw him closer.

'You were how old?'

They were both whispering, the words disappearing into the darkness of the hut.

'Five, from what I've pieced together and what Hallie found out when they took me in. Yet the sight of him with his raised arm lives with me day and night. It's there inside me, Emma, the same way as his genes are. I know I have his temper, I've felt it surge inside me from time to time—quick, hot, unthinking—and I wouldn't want to put someone I love at risk.'

'But Pop was your father for far longer than your birth father was around,' Emma pointed out. 'I know debate rages over nature versus nurture but surely you've been far more influenced by Pop than by your birth father.'

'In every way except genetically,' he argued, then he drew back from her. 'Anyway, that's the story. You asked, and now I've told you, okay?'

Only it wasn't okay at all. In fact, Emma wanted to cry. Wanted to hold him in her arms and tell him it was nonsense, that she knew him well enough to know he'd never harm another human being, maybe any living thing. But she sensed he wouldn't listen, and she knew for sure that other people would have tried—Hallie and Pop in particular.

And if Hallie and Pop, who'd raised him and loved him unconditionally, couldn't convince him he was wrong, how was she, who barely knew him, going to succeed?

Although she didn't *barely* know him at all. She might not have known him long, but she did know he was special. He was caring and compassionate, kind, and friendly, and fun to be with. He was special…

CHAPTER NINE

KEN DIED AT three and, swallowing a sob, Emma conscientiously wrote it in her notes. Marty had collected the stretcher from where he'd left it by the door and together they gently lifted the frail body onto it, Emma wrapping the quilt around it this time, as if he could still feel the cold.

They carried him to the chopper and secured the stretcher, then walked together back into the hut, knowing they had to check for any papers he might have, to dispose of any food, blow out the lanterns, and if possible secure the hut against any vandals that might make their way out here.

But the stress of the vigil, their sadness at the old man's death, and Marty's story had churned up too many emotions and in search of relief they turned to each other, clasping each other in a vice-like grip.

Their kiss spread fire through their bodies as they melded together, feeding the hunger that had been raging between them for too long.

Had it gone on forever, or was it only a matter of minutes before Marty eased himself away from Emma?

'Later?' he whispered.

'Later,' she replied, and it sounded like a promise.

He took one of the lamps outside to where he knew Ken had kept a meat-safe in the shade of a lean-to, and emptied it of cheese and some bread that had been there long enough to be breeding different types of mould.

Emma had found garbage bags and had handed one to him, so he emptied the weird metal contraption with the wet bags hung over it, and returned to the shack to find other perishables.

'I've put together all the papers I can find,' Emma told him, for all the world as if this was just another day, another job and the word 'later' had never been said. Twice. 'There should be something there about next-of-kin if he had anyone.'

She paused, then added, frowning slightly, 'Should we take his clothes? There's not much and most of it should be thrown away.'

'I think leave them. Someone will come out to see to things out here.'

'Then I'll sweep the floor to leave it tidy,' she said, and had to smile.

'Putting off the later?' he teased, coming closer to her to touch her cheek.

'No, I'm not!' she snapped. 'Now get out while I sweep.'

He walked down to the creek, pausing where he'd sat with Ken in days gone by, then looked back at the shack.

Had Ken been hiding not from people but from life itself?

Was that what he, Marty, was doing—hiding from life, but doing it amongst people, plenty of people so they didn't realise…?

Emma cleared what she could from the little shack, sadness for the old man she hadn't known battling with Marty's explanation of why he wouldn't—in his mind couldn't—do commitment.

Personally, she was certain nurture played a far more important part in a person's upbringing than nature, but she knew from the way he'd spoken that Marty held a deep, primal fear of physically hurting someone he loved.

She'd done some psychology as part of her medical course, but not enough to know if such a deep-rooted notion could ever be dislodged. Certainly, the love he'd received from Hallie and Pop and the loving support of all his foster family hadn't driven it away, so possibly not.

And *that* thought filled her with unutterable sadness…

'Come on, it's time to go.'

Marty's call woke her to the fact they should be moving, and she gathered the little stack of papers she'd collected, and with a last look around the shack headed for the door.

Only to stop, and turn, aware something had caught her eye, yet unable to place it. She looked around, certain she'd seen something that might be important—just a glimpse—turned again and caught it, an early sunbeam catching on glass, high up on the wall—a photo!

She hurried back and lifted it off the nail where it was hanging, not stopping to investigate as Marty already had the engine revving and she knew she had to go.

Blow out the lamp and go…

But once on the chopper, belted in, she had time to wipe the dust of ages off the glass and take a proper look at the picture in her hands.

A photo of a woman—young, and rather beautiful—beautiful in that haunting way as if the image could be labelled sadness.

It was the eyes—the look in them—that gave that impression—a polite half-smile on lovely lips, but such sadness in the heavy-lidded eyes Emma could feel it in her chest, her heart…

She turned it over, looking for a name, but the back was bare. Yet somehow she was sure she knew this woman.

Or did she only know the feeling the woman portrayed?

Nonsense!

Why should *she* be sad? She had the boys, her father, a job she loved, and she'd made sure over the years to keep her memories of Simon to the happy times.

These she had tucked into that box that she stored in the back of her mind, and if she took it out and sifted through them from time to time, well, that was only natural surely.

But permanent sadness like this woman had been feeling?

The slightest of bumps told her they were back at Base, an ambulance waiting to take Ken's body to the hospital. She'd already learned they only used the hospital landing site for emergencies, sparing patients and staff within the building unnecessary noise disturbance.

She undid the stretcher straps, then stood aside as two ambos came in to take over. She grabbed her bag and clasping the paperwork she'd found—and the photograph—against her chest, she jumped lightly down and walked towards Marty's vehicle.

And now the memory of 'later' returned to the forefront of her mind.

'My place?' he said as he opened the door for her, and she'd probably have said no if he hadn't touched a finger to her chin and lifted her head so he could look into her eyes.

And she into his, so what she saw there took her breath away.

She nodded, and slid in, wanting to be close, to feel his heat and wonder how his skin would feel against hers.

He pulled up in front of a small house, set in a wild cottage garden that would be a riot of colour in the daylight.

'Hallie does my garden,' he said as he helped her out, and she knew they were just words to keep him going until they were inside, because the hand that held hers was shaking, and her own body was tight with tension.

They barely made it through the door before they were kissing again, Emma desperate to learn the taste of him, to run her fingers through his hair, across his back—learning the feel of him, needing all her senses to take in this man, needing to drown in him…

A voice in Marty's head shrieked warnings, but it was too far away to be clearly heard. Emma was so soft in all the right places, so pliant as he moved towards a wall to give them some support, and he knew she needed this as much as he did.

They fumbled with each other's clothes, while their lips maintained a desperate contact. Then her breasts, bare, soft and warm, were pressed against his skin, while her hand had slid down his belly, easing down his jeans, to hold him, hard and hot, in her hands.

He found her heat, already moist, and lifted her so her legs clamped around his waist, and he could slide into her, death adding passion to the frantic coupling—the act an affirmation of life.

She cried out as he groaned his own release, and she eased back against the wall, still clasped in his arms, breathing hard, trembling slightly.

So he held her, her head resting on his shoulder, until the trembling ceased, and his own breathing steadied. Then, for a little longer, for this was Emma, and this *could* not be because—

Because he loved her?

Hadn't he dismissed that thought way back in their friendship?

So why now had he discovered it anew right now?

The idea was so astonishing he shook his head to dislodge it, but the movement did little more than make Emma move in his arms—still close but not so close she couldn't rearrange her clothing and do up the buttons on her shirt.

So, he, too, pulled clothes into place, his fingers not quite steady as the enormity of what he—they—had just done hit him with the force of a boxer's punch.

'I know there's no commitment,' Emma said quietly, moving away from him. 'It was just something we both needed at the time.'

Yet he read pain in her eyes—knew she needed more…

What could he say?

I love you?

Would she feel she had to love him back?

When he knew full well how much love had hurt her in the past, and how she didn't want to risk it?

They walked out to the car.

The short ride home was agony for Emma. She knew she'd want him again—want to make love with him properly next time—want to do it slowly, unhurriedly, delighting in discovering the man inside the clothes, delighting in his discovery of her…

Tiredness, that's all it was. She'd sat beside him in the vehicle often enough without wanting to rip his clothes off, so of course she could sit beside him again.

Would sit beside him again.

Had to sit beside him again…

She looked down at the photo she'd left in the car, seeking distraction in its beauty and sadness.

Had Ken loved her, this woman with the hauntingly sad eyes?

Had *she* loved him in return?

And had their love been doomed, as hers and Marty's was?

Love?

She looked harder at the face in the picture, turning it to show Marty when he got in.

'I found this,' she said, and he took it from her hands to look at it.

'She's lovely,' he said, passing it back, no mention of sad eyes or unrequited love.

'Might have been his mother,' he added.

No, she was too young to have been his mother—the clothing told Emma that much. She'd seen a similar dress in another photo somewhere—a photo of her paternal grandmother perhaps? They'd discovered boxes of old photos when they'd moved into the old house…

She was so engrossed in the distraction she'd provided for herself that she was startled when Marty pulled up at her front gate.

She opened the door and turned to thank him—well, to look at him really but she'd thank him as well.

He was staring straight ahead, his face so still it might have been carved from marble—a bust that was titled, 'Say Nothing'.

She thanked him anyway and slipped out, heading for the gate and, now that she was home, praying that the boys would still be asleep and she could tiptoe into her bedroom and maybe get an hour's rest before they woke.

Puppy—why hadn't they found a real name for the huge dog? Puppy was just ridiculous!—was there to greet her, and she patted him gently then sent him back to his bed on the veranda.

Making it safely to her bedroom was one thing, but she desperately needed a shower, and as the bathroom was close to the boys' room that was hardly an option right now.

'One day I'll put in an en suite bathroom,' she muttered to herself, sinking down onto the bed and flopping back, staring at the ceiling, at the wall opposite her bed, at the portrait of a woman that had hung there when they'd moved in and which she'd decided to leave hanging there.

She sat up, looking more closely, then knew, tired as she was, she'd have to stand up and look more closely.

Standing in front of it, she shook her head, unable to believe the coincidence. The artist had put a glint of laughter in the eyes of the woman as he'd painted her—maybe they'd been talking, joking—but the dress was certainly the same as the one in the photo, and the heavy-lidded eyes were unmistakeable.

She'd always assumed it was a portrait of her great-aunt, the woman who had left the house to her father because she'd never married, never had children of her own.

Because of unrequited love?

Because Ken Irvine hadn't asked her—or had he asked her and been turned down?

Not by her, if the sadness in her eyes in his picture was any guide.

Separated by her family perhaps, so she'd lived on alone, a lonely woman in a large house that should have been filled with children's laughter, while deep in the forest Ken kept her near him in a picture on his wall…

It's all nonsense, she told herself. You're tired and your imagination's gone into overdrive. You should give up doctoring and write romance novels if you can come up with such a story so quickly.

Or was it something else that had fired her imagination?

Had the picture been symbolic of—?

No!

Perhaps?

No!

Although it could be, couldn't it? Symbolic of her and Marty…

Except Marty didn't love her, and she wasn't sure she loved him.

Not definitely sure…

Go to bed!

CHAPTER TEN

OFF DUTY FOR the day, Marty drove carefully back to his little house on the top of the hill.

From the day, aged fourteen, when he'd started work at the local Wetherby surf shop, he'd banked every penny he'd earned—drawing out what he needed for gifts for family members at Christmas or birthdays or sometimes a bunch of flowers for Hallie, but squirrelling the rest away with one aim in mind.

Eventually he'd have enough for a deposit on a house—*his* house, his *home.*

He'd once joked to Mac that he'd learned more maths working out how to get the best interest on his money than he ever had at school.

So why, as he dumped the rubbish bag from Ken's shack into his wheelie bin and walked into his house, did he not feel the usual thrill of possession—the pride of ownership—that the house usually gave him?

Because it was empty?

Ridiculous. *He* was here, wasn't he?

Was it because the air retained a faint scent of Emma?

He shook away *that* memory. It had been something they'd both needed, an affirmation of life—nothing more…

No, it was the house itself that bothered him. It seemed

to echo with the same kind of…not exactly sadness but definitely emptiness as Ken's shack had.

He touched the walls he'd painted with such care, walked through to the kitchen where appliances he'd chosen himself stood neatly on their shelves.

Maybe it was because he was hungry.

He pulled some bacon from the refrigerator and set it under the grill, turning the heat up high so it wouldn't take forever. Made himself a pot of tea—not for him a tea-bag in a cup—he had enough of that at work. No, Hallie had instilled in him that tea came from a pot, pointing out that you could always pour a second cup, or even a third, if you felt like it.

Hallie…

Was Emma right when she talked about nature and nurture?

Hallie and Pop had certainly nurtured him, and taught him not only the skills he'd need to live a successful life but the values to lead a good life.

Which he had—in his own way, right up until Emma Crawford had walked into the picture and everything had become so convoluted in his mind he didn't know where to start thinking about it.

And desperately wanting to make love to her again—to make love, not just have sex—was not the answer.

More a problem that he'd just have to ignore and hope it would go away.

Because, for all the nurturing he'd received, he knew that, in a flash, nature could take over. It hadn't happened for years but it *had* happened, the first time when he'd been at high school and an older boy had been teasing Liane.

He hadn't seen the red mist that he'd read about in books, hadn't seen or heard anything, although he knew there'd been shouting. He'd simply charged in, fists flailing, more missing than connecting but throwing enough lucky ones for the boy to end up with a black eye and a broken nose.

During the weeks he'd been suspended from school, he'd gone to work with Pop, too young to drive the big rig then but keeping him company, and Pop had never once spoken of the incident, just chatted on as Pop did when he was driving, pointing out places of interest, taking Marty to towns he'd never visited before.

But Pop was basically a quiet man, so there had been plenty of silence for Marty's head to think about what had happened, and about his reaction. To think about his father, and worry that he was like him…

And at the end of the two weeks' banishment, Hallie had packed his lunch and put it in his backpack, kissed his cheek, and sent him off with the others as if nothing had ever happened.

Their attitude had confused him and it was only years later that he'd spoken to them about it.

'What could we say that you weren't learning for yourself? You were bright enough to work out you had to find other ways to react, and better ways to protect your family and friends.'

She'd looked at him across the table with its teapot full of endless cups of tea and smiled.

'And you did, didn't you?'

She'd been right. He'd learned to walk away, taking a sibling or friend with him—to turn his back on bullies instead of becoming a bully himself.

Which had been fine until girlfriends had entered his life—and one had left his life for another bloke and—

What had he been?

Eighteen?

And yet he hadn't actually hurt the bloke for all he'd wanted to…

* * *

Emma woke at midday, surprised she'd slept at all, until she read the note Christine had left on the kitchen table.

'We've all gone to Wetherby for the day. Hallie and Pop are cleaning out the attics and have found some toys the boys might like.'

And in a different hand, 'Might make a day of it and bring you back fish and chips for dinner. Love Dad.'

Disappointment shafted through her, though maybe, her practical self told her, it was hunger. But as she made and ate some toast and drank a morning coffee, she did feel a little disappointed that she couldn't talk to her father about the photo and the portrait on her wall.

She'd checked it again when she'd got up—holding the two close together—and she was sure they were images of the same woman.

But who?

The great-aunt she'd never met?

She phoned Carrie, but got an answering-machine and assumed she'd probably gone on the jaunt to Wetherby as well. The people carrier she and Dad had bought when she'd been expecting the twins would certainly hold everyone.

And leave room for toys.

Anyway, Carrie would be too young to know much. Someone's grandmother, that's who she'd need to find.

Joss?

Joss's mother had produced Christine, and Emma still had the phone number.

But what to say?

Do you know the woman in this photo?

Surely that would be far too personal—and too intrusive because, dead or not, she'd still be meddling in Ken Irvine's affairs.

She sighed, deciding to give up thinking about the photo at least until she'd talked to her father…

But not thinking about the photo created a vacuum in her mind and, naturally enough, into it rushed the other revelations of the night.

If she thought only about Marty's story—about his mother's death—and his determination not to risk hurting anyone he loved, maybe she'd forget what had happened later.

Hardly possible as her body tingled just *not* remembering it.

She'd go to work. That would stop her thinking about anything outside the job at hand. And although she had no idea just how her work roster stood at the moment, never having worked out how the rescue helicopter hours fitted into the general work timetable, there'd always be something she could do, even if it meant attacking the mountains of paperwork that multiplied on her desk in the small office she shared with the other ED doctors.

Except Marty was the first person she saw when she walked in.

'What are *you* doing here?' she demanded, before realising he was surrounded by young men and women and she'd embarrassed herself far more than she'd embarrassed him.

'Ah, Emma, just the person we needed,' he said, with such a bland smile she wanted to hit him. 'These are a group of medical students from Retford university. We always take some for work experience so they can see a smaller hospital in action, and although we don't wish for accidents it's an opportunity for them to see how the search and rescue team operates.'

Emma smiled feebly at the four young women and two young men who made up the group.

'Emma,' Marty continued, 'usually joins the rescue team when we have a callout that requires a doctor.'

'And is she trained the way you say you're trained?' one of the young women asked, flashing such a dazzling smile at Marty Emma wanted to hit her.

Or *him,* for he was smiling right back at the questioner, all daring charm.

'Of course,' he said. 'We had a training day only last week. Every member of the team has to update their skills twice a year.'

The young woman looked as if she'd have liked to have been at the training day, and Marty's smile suggested he wouldn't have minded at all, but one of the men was now asking, 'Don't most SAR teams have their own doctors on staff? Wouldn't it be better carrying a doctor who knows what he's doing?'

He realised what he'd said, blushed, and turned to Emma.

'Sorry, ma'am, that came out wrong.'

'Indeed it did,' Marty replied, not bothering to hide his delight at both Emma's and the young man's embarrassment. 'But we're a very small operation, situated at a small country hospital because from here we can cover a far wider range than we would flying out of Retford, for example. Originally this service was connected to the Lifesaver's movement with sponsorship from big business, and we still get that sponsorship, although we get some government help as well.'

'So all doctors here at Braxton can be on call?' the young man persisted, and Emma took pity on him.

'In areas where there are no doctors employed by search and rescue operations the local doctors, usually from the emergency department, are used. I think one of the reasons I got this job was because I'd been trained for SAR missions, and had done winch training, underwater rescue, which is great fun if ever you want to get into SAR, rescues off moving targets like ships at sea, the lot.'

The young man looked at her in admiration.

'I wish we'd been here for that training day you had, it sounds like fun.'

Emma's eyes met Marty's across the young heads, and the slight nod he gave told her that he, too, was thinking of Ken. But they were young and idealistic, these students, and didn't really need to know about sitting by someone's bed waiting for them to die when all your years of training and experience had been about helping people live…

A wave of tiredness swept over her and she knew she'd have been better off staying at home and trying to sleep, no matter what thoughts would have run in circles through her head.

'Will you join us for lunch? We're just off to continue this discussion in the canteen then we're taking the hospital bus out to the base to show them around.'

Emma would have loved to say no, but there'd been the hint of a plea in Marty's voice, and if he felt as tired as she was feeling, he would need help to field the students' questions.

The young man who'd asked the question—Alex, she'd discovered—made sure he sat next to her at the long table, and Emma smiled to herself as she saw the young women crowd around Marty.

Like moths to a flame, she thought, and realised that, quite apart from his commitment problems, he would be a dangerous man to know well because he *was* kind and interesting and always willing to help, but anyone who loved him would live in a constant state of jealousy which would surely eat away at the strongest relationship.

Anyone who loved him?

No, no, she *definitely* didn't.

Couldn't!

So why was she probably turning green as he patted a beautiful young blonde on the hand?

Why did her stomach scrunch when he smiled at the hot brunette?

Damn the man! He'd bewitched her. He'd made it quite clear right from the start—and had definitely confirmed it last night—that he wasn't available for any kind of commitment, then he'd taken her with a passion that had imprinted him not only in her mind but on her body.

The problem was that she'd responded with equal intensity and although she had known full well it had been nothing more than just sex, her body tingled even thinking about it.

CHAPTER ELEVEN

THE STUDENT GROUP, and Alex in particular, begged her to come out to the SAR base with them, but she pleaded work and hurried back to the ED. She knew, given time, she'd get over the heart lurches and galloping pulse every time she saw Marty, but until that happened, avoidance was definitely the answer.

Sylvie greeted her with relief.

'We're having one of those days when it's dead quiet for an hour, then everyone comes at once. Could you see a lass in cubicle one who's complaining of stomach cramps?'

Emma was only too glad to be occupied, and she made her way to the cubicle where a very young woman, a teenager, in fact, was crying copiously into a handful of paper tissues the nurse on duty had given her.

The lass was very overweight and was probably bullied mercilessly at school.

The nurse introduced Ebony to Emma, then muttered something about work to do and departed, so Emma helped the still-crying patient onto the examination table.

Even under layers of clothing unsuited to the warm weather, once Ebony was lying supine, a possible cause of the stomach cramps became obvious.

Not wanting to cause further distress, Emma checked Ebony's blood pressure—good—pulse, a bit rapid but no cause for concern, and took some blood for testing—*and* typing, although she didn't say that out loud.

She was feeling Ebony's swollen stomach when the girl yowled in pain.

Emma held her hand, noted the time, then said gently, 'Did you know you were pregnant?'

Colour drained from Ebony's face, leaving it as white as the pillow case.

'Dad'll kill me,' she said, and Emma closed her eyes momentarily in a silent *Please don't let it be Dad* prayer.

'Do you have a boyfriend?'

A miserable nod of the head.

'Once I did but then he was just like the others and laughed and called me Fatty.'

'But you had sex with him?' Emma was watching the clock as she spoke—the contractions, for that was surely what they had been, were still widely spaced.

'Only a couple of times.' The defensive reply must have brought unwanted memories for Ebony began to cry again.

She felt Ebony's abdomen, finding the shape of the foetus, then, speaking quietly, she explained she'd have to examine her.

The nurse had reappeared, and together they removed Ebony's jeans and knickers.

Even a quick glance showed the cervix had begun to dilate. This baby was coming.

'The cramps are telling us the baby is on the way. It will be a while yet—' please let it not be too long, her head whispered '—so is there someone you'd like to have with you. What about your mum?'

Hope battled the tears in Ebony's eyes.

'Do you think she'd come?' she asked. 'She'll be mad at me, you see. She mightn't want to come.'

'Would you like me to phone her and explain?' Emma asked, then watched the emotions play across Ebony's face.

Mum would be mad, but she did want Mum, but then Mum would tell Dad, although Mum could usually fix Dad when he was angry. They were as easy to read as the pages of a book.

Finally, Ebony nodded, and Emma took the file with the name and address on it so she could phone the mother, leaving Ebony with the nurse.

'The cramps?' Sylvie asked. 'Is she pregnant?'

Emma nodded. 'Could you arrange to have her taken up to Maternity, while I phone her mother? Poor woman, although maybe she's had her suspicions.'

Sylvie was already on the house phone, arranging the transfer, so Emma made the call from the privacy of her office.

Mrs Challoner, Ebony's mum, was not nearly as surprised as her daughter.

'I kept thinking maybe that was it,' she said, 'but at that age they hate you asking questions and with all the sex education they get at school I thought she'd know if she was—or even suspected it—and she'd talk to me.'

'I'm sorry,' Emma said. 'But perhaps she didn't know. If she's usually a bit irregular she probably put it down to that then forgot all about it.'

'Or was so terrified she shut it right out of her mind,' Mrs Challoner said, a break in her voice telling Emma how upset she was—not, Emma thought, about the pregnancy, but about Ebony not talking to her.

'I'll be right up,' the anxious mother said. 'Where will I find her?'

'Come to the emergency department. We're transferring her to Maternity but it sometimes takes time and if she's still here, she'll be happier going up there with you than on her own.'

'Bless you,' Mrs Challoner said. 'I'll be there as soon as I can.'

Bless you.

What a lovely thing for someone to have said, Emma thought as she made her way back to Ebony to assure her that her mother was on the way.

Two words—but enough to reassure Emma too. This mother would stand by her child and probably bring up her grandchild.

And for a moment she wondered what it would have been like to grow up with a mother.

She shook the thought away. Dad had done his best to be both mother and father to her, and as far as she was concerned he'd done a damned good job.

But would her boys grow up and wonder what it might have been like to have had a father?

Should she get serious about finding a father for them?

Somehow that task seemed slightly distasteful now.

It was all Marty's fault…

Marty had finished with the students and was back in Ken's shack, flying out in his own chopper on what should have been time off. The old man had prided himself on keeping it clean, but he'd probably been failing for some time, and Marty wanted to make sure it was as spruce as Ken would have had it in the early days.

Yet walking in brought memories of Emma—of her closeness as they'd sat waiting for the old man to die, of her softness later when they'd found relief from the trauma that came with any death, back at his house…

He cleared and cleaned almost maniacally, aware his burst of energy was a way of not remembering. And when he was finally happy that Ken's little home looked as it had when the old man had been younger, he went out into the bush, picking red gum tips and yellow bottlebrush, dark green fig leaves and some trailing creeper.

He arranged them all in a big old coffee can, just as

Ken had done, and set them in the empty fireplace. They'd dry out there, and still look good—a dried arrangement, Hallie had told him they were called.

He checked the cleared area around the shack for rubbish and loaded it all into the chopper.

Then he walked towards the little creek that gurgled and splashed its way down the mountain, and sat on the log where he had sat at least a dozen times with Ken, listening to his stories of the bush, picking up a lot of the older man's ideas about life and how to live it—about being true to oneself, and owing nothing to any man.

And love?

Thinking back, he couldn't remember discussing love with Ken, although he'd been there often as a teenager when love—or more probably lust—had never been far from his thoughts.

'What would you have said, Ken?' he asked of the man who was no longer there.

But try as he might, Marty couldn't imagine what Ken's response would have been, and as the creek had nothing to tell him either, he walked back to shut the door of the shack and took himself, reluctantly, back to Braxton.

Reluctantly because he was off duty and being off duty gave him more time to think, and while he might now be out of the shack and his memories of Ken's life, the fact remained that he'd had unprotected sex with the one woman in the world he would hate to hurt.

Maybe it would be okay…

She was looking for a father for her boys, so she was probably on the Pill…

Surely she was on the Pill?

Yet, somehow, he was pretty sure she wasn't.

Emma was too organised, too methodical, to look beyond going out with any possible candidates in her quest.

She was conservative, would take it slowly, not rush into anything—

Which meant she'd go on the Pill when she was ready to commit to a man, not take it all the time just in case.

Concentrate on flying, he told himself, but he knew he could fly this little toy in his sleep.

Nevertheless, he did concentrate, more to block out the other thoughts, and he landed at the base, carried the rubbish bags to the skip, cleaned out and refuelled the chopper, and even gave it a wash.

'Too much time on your hands?' Dave called to him. 'You can help me do a stocktake, then while I clean out the chopper you can take the list to the hospital and bring back the stock.'

No way! He was avoiding the hospital.

Only surely Emma wouldn't be there—not after pulling an all-nighter.

And he *did* need something to do.

Emma had sent her patient up to Maternity, put staples into the split head of a teenager, and dug a bead from the nose of a kindergarten kid.

Deciding, as she wasn't supposed to be on duty that day, she could have a cup of tea, she escaped to the tearoom, desperate to have a think.

Why hadn't it occurred to her earlier?

Why did she have to wait until a pregnant teenager came in before she considered her own situation, and the fact that she'd had unprotected sex with the one man in the world she shouldn't have?

But her mind grew cloudy so thinking of the possible consequences got muddled up with the remembered warmth—no, heat—the act had brought with it.

She made a mug of tea, grabbed a couple of biscuits from the never-empty tin, and sat down to muse.

Well, to think really, mostly about consequences of actions, but there was more musing than thinking going on.

Marty's arrival put paid to both. Her mind went blank and she could only stare at him.

'You shouldn't be here,' he said, and she recovered enough to point out, 'Neither should you.'

Then he was sitting on the sofa beside her, close but not too close—annoyingly not too close, but she wouldn't think about that either.

'Oh, Em,' he said, and even the shortening of her name made her feel warm. 'I'm so sorry. I didn't think, I didn't ask— Hell, what if—?'

She put her hand on his knee, wishing he was closer, knowing the wish was stupid.

'It's as much my fault as yours, and it's highly unlikely that there'll be any fallout so don't worry about it.'

'Not worry about it?'

His voice had risen and she touched her finger to his lips to hush him, then grew hot and breathless as he slid his tongue along it and closed his lips against the tip, sucking it gently.

It took a mammoth effort but she finally removed it.

'We can't do this,' she said, and if she sounded desperate, well, that was just how she felt.

He shifted, nodded, shrugged, stood up, then reached down to touch her cheek.

'You *will* tell me if you're pregnant,' he said, his voice harsh with an emotion she couldn't read.

She nodded, not at all sure she would.

If it happened, and that was one huge if, she'd think about it then—think about what was to be done, what would be the best way forward. But not today. It would be like when Simon had been dying and she would only let herself think of one day at a time.

Although that had been totally different—back then it had been death she'd been desperately trying to hold off.

But life?

A new life?

She had no idea how she'd feel about that.

CHAPTER TWELVE

EMMA HAD PUT the possibility of being pregnant completely out of her mind, and tried, unsuccessfully, to do the same with Marty.

He seemed to be around more than usual, bobbing up in the tea-room at unexpected times, coming in with a patient when usually Mark and Dave would bring them in.

So, a week or two later, when she heard the helicopter fly over—its distinctive noise far too recognisable by now—she fully expected to see him when it returned. The gossip in A and E was something about a road giving way—the result of the rain they'd had during the week after the bushfires causing a landslide effect.

She was hearing snippets of theories about why this sometimes happened, but not really taking much notice as it was a busy morning.

Until Mark walked in, with a list of equipment and drugs needed for restocking.

'You not on the chopper for the landslide mission?' she asked.

'Kicked off by Marty,' he said. 'Matt's flying, and Dave will act as winch man. Marty wants to go down.'

'Marty wants to go down?' Emma repeated the words as ice-cold fear swept through her body.

'He's still a qualified paramedic—jolly good one too—

but he knew he was a better pilot than anyone else around here when we first got the chopper, so he took it on.'

'But why would he choose to go down now?' she asked, although she already knew the answer.

The rescue must be tricky, probably dangerous, and knowing Marty now, she also knew he wouldn't let his crew put their lives at risk.

And definitely not crew with families.

'Where is it? What's happened?' she demanded of Mark, when he'd ignored her first question.

'Out on an old timber road. Some new folks have recently bought a property out that way and want to turn it into a holiday camp for children—you know, farm animals and horse riding and milking cows.'

But Emma couldn't care less about the cows right now, or the new people.

'Apparently,' Mark continued, 'Pop was taking out a load of cattle for them. These days he only does the odd job like a small mob of cattle, or sometimes in his covered trailer a load of furniture for someone. As far as I know, the road slid out from under his cabin in the prime mover and he's stuck there, with the cabin of the prime mover balanced over the edge of the slide, the trailer weight and cattle the only thing holding it from plunging down the slope.'

Mark was still talking but somehow Emma's mind had stopped at the word 'Pop'. That's why Marty was going down the wire. Of course he would, with Pop in danger.

She *had* to be there.

Had to be sure he was safe…

She looked frantically around the ER—not busy but it could be any moment. She checked her watch. Still an hour before she was off duty. She checked the rosters. Paul was taking over from her and she knew, since his return to full-time work, he was always looking for overtime.

She phoned him, told him what was happening, and although she had no way to explain why she needed to be at the accident, he seemed pleased enough to cover for her.

'Be there in ten,' he said, and she blessed the closeness of everything in the small town.

By the time he arrived she'd found out exactly where the landslide had occurred and how to get there.

She raced home and was thankful to see their car was out front. Dad and the kids were probably down at the park. Once inside, she wrote a note explaining where she'd be, changed into jeans and boots, a tough checked shirt, and headed off towards the collapsed road.

She knew she shouldn't be doing this, because onlookers—and that's all she'd be—were a nuisance at any accident, to say nothing of what havoc vehicles could cause on an already weakened road.

A police car blocked the road long before she could see anything, except the helicopter hovering above the trees further ahead.

'You can't go further, miss,' the policeman told her.

Emma hesitated for a second, then told her lie—a small lie but a lie nonetheless.

'I'm a doctor, I was told I might be needed.'

'You'll have to walk and it's a good mile, uphill most of the way.'

As if that mattered. She just had to be there.

She thanked the man, then, sneaking past, off the road now and through the bush above it, she eventually saw the back of Pop's truck.

But the scene that eventually met her eyes was horrifying.

The cabin of the vehicle hung precariously, tilted downwards, over nothingness. The cattle in the trailer were restless, and getting increasingly so, making the prime mover shake, but it was obvious to Emma that if they were removed, the loss of their weight would send the whole thing plunging into the gully.

As well as police cars and fire service vehicles closer to the accident, she saw a large crane, although that had apparently been stopped from moving closer for fear its weight would make things on the unstable road worse. Men were uncoiling a thick wire from the crane, maybe intending to hook it to the rear of the truck as extra anchoring weight.

But more horrifying than all of it—the dangling truck, the increasingly restless cattle—was the sight of Marty, in his flight suit, half in and half out of the cabin.

Emma crept closer, unable to stop herself, willing the man she loved—yes, okay, that was finally sorted out—to stay safe.

Was Pop wedged in there somehow that it was taking so long to get him out?

A rumble beneath her feet gave warning that time was running out, and the rest of the road was about to follow the earlier slide into the gully. She could hear Marty's voice but it was too muffled to hear the words, so she stood, hands clasped tightly, lips firmly shut so she didn't make a noise and distract him.

Reaching Pop had been no trouble at all. Matt was holding the hover well, and he, Marty, had missed the worst of the tall timber branches on the way down but now Marty couldn't work out how to extricate his father.

He'd leaned far enough in to release his seatbelt, but the old man—his dearly loved Pop—was only semi-conscious—shock possibly—and could do little to help.

Trapped as he was in the cabin, there was no way Marty could get a strop around him, so it would have to be a manual lift. The problem was, the door was jammed so it meant hauling a solidly built, seventy-something-year-old man through the window.

And a dead weight at that.

If he got a firm hold on Pop, and asked them to unload the cattle, the truck would plunge down the gully, and he could lift Pop free as it fell.

Or, and it was a big or, the combined weight of himself, Pop and the truck could pull the helicopter down with it, crashing it into the trees.

Couldn't risk it.

He kicked at the door, more in frustration than in hope he might shift it, and to his surprise it flew open, Pop tumbling out.

Dave on the winch must have seen what had happened and dropped Marty lower, so he was able to grab at the only father he'd ever really known and hang on tight, wrapping his arms and his legs around Pop's unresponsive body.

He signaled to lift, and as they rose said to Pop, 'If you can, hang onto me, that way we'll be doubly safe.'

But shock and maybe a head knock when the cabin tilted had the old man out cold.

They rose slowly with the double weight, the wire twisting so Marty thought he caught a glimpse of Emma by the roadside.

He couldn't look again, his full attention needed to get Pop to safety. Then Dave was there to haul them up onto the skids, checking Marty was okay before dragging Pop into the chopper.

Marty crawled in himself, unhooking from the winch wire, fingers trembling now he realised just how close run it had been, his body shaking from the strain of the lift.

Below them they could see the cattle being unloaded, then hear, above the engine noise, the roar as the land beneath the road plunged into the gully.

He strapped in and sat there, trying hard to quell his tremors, while Dave settled Pop on the stretcher, the old man now awake and complaining that he was perfectly well and didn't need Dave's fussing.

But Marty was trying to remember what he'd seen. It couldn't have been Emma.

Could it?

Or had he conjured her up because he'd been thinking of her—thinking of Pop, of fatherhood, and right along that train of thought to Emma and the boys.

With relief battling rage within her, Emma drove back to town as fast as she dared on the winding mountain road.

Hospital or base?

Surely they'd take Pop to the hospital to have him checked over, although she knew Marty would prefer the base, where he could see to the old man himself.

The chopper was so far in front of her when she cleared the trees she couldn't see it, but decided to go straight to the base.

And there he was, helping Pop down out of the side door, steadying him as they walked across to the hut, talking, talking—probably questioning him about how he felt.

Emma stayed in the car and waited, aware she didn't belong here—shouldn't be here—should be anywhere but here, really…

But she had to see him, touch him, make sure he was all right, so there she stayed.

He must have seen the car for eventually he walked towards it. She got out as he drew nearer, knowing the metal walls around her weren't enough to contain her rage.

'Emma, what are you—?'

'What in heaven's name did you think you were doing?' she yelled at him, before he had time to complete his question. 'You could have been killed! Eventually they'd have got a wire attached to the back of the truck and hauled it backwards, there was no need for you to put your life in danger like that. You frightened me to death.'

'Or the road could have given way first,' he said quietly, touching her shoulder.

One touch and the rage abated, leaving her feeling so weak she wanted—no, needed—to lean against him, to feel him against her, to be one with him as surely they were meant to be.

And perhaps he felt the same as he folded his arms around her, held her close, dropping kisses on the top of her head.

'I'm sorry you were frightened,' he murmured, 'but...'

He paused and moved a little away from her, one finger tilting her chin so he could look into her face.

'But how could I expect you to accept me as a father to your children if I could not save my own father?'

She pulled away from him, anger rising again within her.

Anger and something else.

Hope?

'What did you say?' she demanded, looking into the blue eyes she knew so well.

Smiling now, though warily...

'I'm asking you to marry me—if you'll have me. Asking because I love you—I think I've loved you from the day we met. But I was so hung up on the past, on my birth father, I resisted it with all my strength, but I can't resist it now. You were right, Pop's my real father, and a better role model no man could ever have. I realised that today when I thought I might lose him. And if I lost him, would I lose you? Or would you marry me out of pity? So many thoughts, Em, but all of them of love.'

He paused, then added, fairly tentatively for someone who'd been talking non-stop, '*Will* you marry me?'

Emma stared at him, trying desperately to assimilate all she'd heard, but the only words that meant something were the early ones, the 'I love you' ones. Words she'd never expected, hardly even dared hope she'd hear on Marty's lips.

She smiled and shook her head, and had moved closer to kiss him when her head shake obviously bothered him.

'You're saying no?'

'That was disbelief,' she said, smiling as she put her arms around him. 'Disbelief that you'd love me when I've only recently realised just how much I love you. I was so afraid, you see. Afraid of love—of loving again. I thought if I made it all about the boys…'

'It wouldn't hurt?' he whispered.

And he held her close again, so they only broke apart at heavy footsteps approaching, and Pop's gruff voice saying, 'If it's all the same to you two, I'd like to get home sometime today. Hallie will be worrying.'

'You can't go home!' They spoke together, then Marty took Emma's hand and he said, 'You need to go to the hospital to be checked out, probably kept in for a while in case you have concussion. *We'll* take you there.'

'Hmph!' Pop said, looking at the pair of them hand in hand in front of him. 'Hallie reckoned this would happen. I just hoped you wouldn't be so stubborn as to not see what a gem you'll have in Emma.'

He smiled at Emma then leaned forward and kissed her cheek.

'He gives you any trouble, my girl, you come straight to me. I've been sorting him out anytime these past thirty years!'

And Emma laughed, and hugged the man who was to become her father-in-law, then Marty took her hand and they headed for her car.

In the end, she dropped them both off at the hospital

and went home to tell her father what was happening—and to ask about the woman in the photo.

'That's your great-aunt,' he said. 'The woman who left us the house.'

'Do you know her story? Did she ever marry?'

Her father frowned, thinking back.

'No, she didn't, but I seem to remember there was a man, someone who felt he wasn't right for her.'

'No wonder her eyes look so sad,' she said, thinking how close she'd come to having that same sadness in her eyes.

When Marty arrived, determined, it appeared, to ask her father's permission for her hand, she waited until the excitement was all over and they were sitting on the veranda on their own.

She showed him the two photos, and told him the story.

'Bloody hell!' he said. 'To think that could have been us if I hadn't finally come to my senses.'

Emma laughed.

'It wouldn't have been us,' she said. 'You once told me I should want a man for myself, not just for the boys, and it took me a little while to accept that. Until I realised that, more than anything, I only wanted—still want, and will always want—you.'

He kissed her then and she relaxed into the kiss, glad they'd not only found each other but had finally found their way to love.

EPILOGUE

THE WHOLE FAMILY was gathered, Lila and Tariq flying in laden with gifts for everyone, Steve and Fran were up from Sydney with their baby Chloe, Carrie and the twins, all three looking beautiful, Izzy and Mac, with George, usually held in Nikki's arms, the centre of much attention as the very latest addition to the family.

Emma and Marty had decided, after much deliberation, to hold the celebration at the old nunnery where the Halliday family—as the locals called them—had grown up.

And there were dozens of them, all present to see the last of the brood safely married off.

Emma dressed in the little flat Pop had fixed up for Izzy when she'd brought Nikki home from hospital—Nikki, the birth daughter of Liane, the sister who hadn't survived her horrendous early childhood.

And Dad was with her in the flat, helping with the last-minute touches, fastening the pearls he'd given her as a wedding gift—pearls that had been his mother's.

'Why didn't my mother take them?' Emma asked, and watched him closely for they rarely spoke of her mother.

'She felt they were yours,' he said. 'She wasn't bad, or uncaring, Emma, she was just a square peg in a round hole and she had to escape or die. She loved you and in her own way loved me, but once she'd met Helena and realised what true love was, she couldn't live a lie anymore.

Helena took her back to Europe, to Hungary where she was from, and from there they roved the world—or that had been the plan when they departed.'

'She never thought to keep in touch?'

Her father drew her close and hugged her, heedless of creases in the soft green dress Emma was wearing.

'She said that that would make it too hard for all three of us, and she was probably right, for it would have awoken memories that hurt both of us.'

He paused, then added, 'Have you missed her?'

Emma eased away from him and looked into his eyes. 'Not for a minute. You've been all I've ever needed and more as far as parents go.'

She kissed his cheek.

'Now, let's go and get this wedding over with,' he said. 'Knowing Hallie, she will have organised a tremendous spread, and everyone will be getting hungry.'

They walked down the stairs and out into the big back yard, where Marty and his family would have played so often. And the family had obviously been busy, for the rather saggy old grape arbour had been fixed and covered with fresh flowers, and a carpet laid beneath it.

And there was Marty, waiting for her, Stephen beside him as support, while Hallie held the hands of two little boys, dressed in smart new clothes for the occasion, Puppy, with flowers in his collar, sitting docilely beside them.

'It's Mummy,' Xavier yelled, and everyone turned to watch her and Dad walk towards them, the two boys, obviously under strict instructions from Hallie, standing very still.

It was Marty who'd insisted they be part of the wedding party, because, as he'd explained, he was marrying all three of them. Well, four of them it would be by the end of the year—but only she and Marty knew that.

And in that flowery bower, looking out over the town towards the sea, they committed to each other, repeating words that echoed down through the mists of time, yet still had the power to bring tears to the eyes of the onlookers.

'You may kiss the bride,' the celebrant declared at last, and as Marty bent to kiss her, the boys broke free, rushing towards Emma, who knelt to hug them both, before Marty lifted them, one on each arm, and turned to his family and all their friends.

'My new family,' he said, and the pride in his voice, and the promise it held, made Emma smile through blurry eyes.

* * * * *

MILLS & BOON

Coming soon

BOUND TO THE
SICILIAN'S BED
Sharon Kendrick

Rocco was going to kiss her and after everything she'd just said, Nicole knew she needed to stop him. But suddenly she found herself governed by a much deeper need than preserving her sanity, or her pride. A need and a hunger which swept over her with the speed of a bush fire. As Rocco's shadowed face lowered towards her she found past and present fusing, so that for a disconcerting moment she forgot everything except the urgent hunger in her body. Because hadn't her Sicilian husband always been able to do this—to captivate her with the lightest touch and to tantalise her with that smouldering look of promise? And hadn't there been many nights since they'd separated when she'd woken up, still half fuddled with sleep, and found herself yearning for the taste of his lips on hers just one more time? And now she had it.

One more time.

She opened her mouth—though afterwards she would try to convince herself she'd been intending to resist him—but Rocco used the opportunity to fasten his mouth over hers in the most perfects of fits. And Nicole felt instantly helpless—caught up in the powerful snare of a sexual mastery which wiped out everything else. She gave a gasp of pleasure because it had been so long since she had done this.

Since they'd been apart Nicole had felt like a living statue—as if she were made from marble—as if the flesh and blood part of her were some kind of half-forgotten dream. Slowly but surely she had withdrawn from the sensual side of her nature, until she'd convinced herself she was dead and unfeeling inside. But here came Rocco to wake her dormant sexuality with nothing more than a single kiss. It was like some stupid fairy story. It was scary and powerful. She didn't *want* to want him, and yet . . .

She wanted him.

Her lips opened wider as his tongue slid inside her mouth—eagerly granting him that intimacy as if preparing the way for another. She began to shiver as his hands started to explore her—rediscovering her body with an impatient hunger, as if it were the first time he'd ever touched her.

'Nicole,' he said unevenly and she'd never heard him say her name like that before.

Her arms were locked behind his neck as again he circled his hips in unmistakable invitation and, somewhere in the back of her mind, Nicole could hear the small voice of reason imploring her to take control of the situation. It was urging her to pull back from him and call a halt to what they were doing. But once again she ignored it. Against the powerful tide of passion, that little voice was drowned out and she allowed pleasure to shimmer over her skin.